THE GOOD VIBRATIONS® GUIDE

THE G-SPOT

Cathy Winks

Down There Press
San Francisco

The Good Vibrations® Guide: The G-Spot

Library of Congress Cataloging-in-Publication Data
Winks, Cathy.
    The Good Vibrations guide : the G-spot / Cathy Winks.
        p.   cm.
    Includes bibliographical references.
    ISBN 0-940208-23-7 (pbk.)
    1. Sex instruction. 2. Women--Sexual behavior. 3. Sex.
    4. Sexual excitement. 5. G spot. I. Title.
    HQ31.W77344   1998
    613.9'6--dc21   97-49060
                                                        CIP
We also offer librarians an Alternative CIP prepared by Sanford Berman,
Head Cataloger at Hennepin County Library, Minnetonka MN, which
may more fully reflect this book's scope and content.

Alternative Cataloging-in-Publication Data
Winks, Cathy, 1960-
    The Good Vibrations guide: the G-spot. San Francisco, CA: Down
There Press, copyright 1998.
    (Good Vibrations guides)
    PARTIAL CONTENTS: Just the facts, ma'm. Clitoris. Urethra and
urethral sponge. Vagina. Anus and perineal sponge. -Nothing new under
the sun. Vaginal erogenous zones. Female prostate. Female fluids.
-Exploration. Communication. How to hit the spot. All about ejacula-
tion. -Tips, toys and techniques. About the PC muscle. About "G-spot
orgasms." Toys. Vibrators. Dildos. -References. -Resources. Bibliography.
Videography. Toys and information.
    1. G-spot. 2. Orgasm, Female. 3. Vulva. 4. Female ejaculation. 5.
Dildos. 6. Vibrators. 7. G-spot--Bibliography. 8. G-spot--Videography.
9. Sex manuals. 10. Sex education for women. I. Title. II. Title: G-spot.
III. Series. IV. Down There Press. V. Good Vibrations, San Francisco,
California.

612.6

Cover Design: MB Condon
Design and Production: Jennifer Wong
Illustration p.4 by MB Condon. Reprinted with permission from *The
New Good Vibrations Guide to Sex,* by Cathy Winks and Anne Semans
(San Francisco: Cleis Press, 1997).

Additional copies of this book are available from your local bookstore or
directly from the publisher:
Down There Press, 938 Howard St., #101, San Francisco CA 94103
Please enclose $11.00 for each copy ordered, which includes postage and
handling.

Printed in the United States of America   18 17 16 15 14 13 12 11 10

Acknowledgments

Thanks to Genanne Walsh, Joani Blank, and Leigh Davidson for their expert editing; to Eric Albert for providing a copy of the Kinsey Institute's bibliography on this subject; and to Gary Schubach for providing information about his doctoral research project, as well as several relevant articles.

Special thanks to Beverly Whipple, a pioneering researcher in women's sexuality. She and her colleagues Alice Kahn Ladas, Harold Ladas and John D. Perry put the G-spot on the map and into the dictionary. Her generous assistance in providing relevant articles, clarifying research and reviewing the manuscript for accuracy was invaluable and hugely appreciated. Needless to say, any mistakes that remain are my own.

Table of Contents

Introduction

One of the guiding philosophies at Good Vibrations is that people's sexual tastes and responses are as individual as their tastes in food, music or the temperature of their bath water. Just as there's no "right" way to cook a meal, there's no "right" way to experience sexual arousal or orgasm.

This philosophy is particularly relevant to any discussion of the G-spot and female ejaculation. These simple sexual phenomena have inspired both a considerable amount of misinformation and a truly stunning degree of media hype. Thanks to the success of the 1982 book *The G Spot: And Other Recent Discoveries About Human Sexuality*, hundreds of thousands of women and their partners have gone fishin' for what the book's back-cover copy dubbed "the vaginal orgasmic trigger," which promised to deliver "a pleasure so intense it will add a whole new dimension to your life."

That's the kind of marketing that makes a book a best seller and fuels thousands of magazine articles laden with exclamation points. Yet, once you get down to the fine print, the authors of *The G Spot* readily acknowledge that some women experience the G-spot as an erogenous zone and others don't; that some women ejaculate and others don't. They were motivated to write their book to affirm aspects of female sexuality that were recognized in folk wisdom and medical science for centuries, but have been dismissed and denied by doctors and sexologists in the modern era. As one sociologist writing on the subject notes, "historically, we have discovered, ignored, and rediscovered biological capacities of women that relate to their sexuality."[1]

There's nothing new under the sun when it comes to human sexuality, and how could there be? What change are our cultural mores and attitudes about how sex and sexuality are defined. In this book, we present everything we know about the G-spot and female ejaculation, much of which we learned from the women and men who shared their personal experiences with us by taking the time to fill out our survey. You'll find excerpts from these surveys throughout the book—we hope you'll find them as enlightening and entertaining as we did.

Accurate information on the G-spot and female ejaculation is still in short supply; most medical texts and sex manuals either avoid or dismiss these topics. It's entirely possible that if you were to report experiences of female ejaculation to your doctor, he or she would tell you you're suffering from urinary incontinence. You may feel like these Good Vibrations customers:

I really, really wish I had known about female ejaculation sooner. I'm 39 and still discovering things about sexuality in general and my own responses in particular. But I'm glad to have finally found out about this.

G-spot stimulation is my very favorite way to be stimulated and have orgasms, period!!! I totally love it—it has changed my sex life and sexual experience in the same way that finding my clit did when I was younger.

If what you read in these pages expands your sexual horizons, that's great. However, we implore you to resist approaching G-spot awareness and female ejaculation as competitive events in some sexual triathalon. We live in such a "how-to" and "fix-it" culture, it can be difficult to simply celebrate our unique sexual reponses, rather than striving to somehow "improve" them.

When I try to stimulate my G-spot, it feels like I'm "missing" it, just slightly uncomfortable. I end up giving up and feeling let down that I didn't find a great new thing about my vagina.

We don't believe that every woman *should* enjoy G-spot stimulation, any more than every man *should* enjoy prostate stimulation; and we certainly haven't found any evidence to the assertion that "any woman can" ejaculate. Whether or not the tips in this book lead you to discover new erogenous zones, we encourage you to adopt a spirit of fun and adventure and just enjoy the ride.

I think that it's like anything else with our bodies: we're all different and have different responses. I think that if you find the G-spot, great, and if not, then that's okay too. It shouldn't be this intensive "I must find it!" sort of thing.

Just the Facts, Ma'am

Before we tackle the who, what, where and when of the G-spot, let's review the basics of female genital anatomy. As you read the following, bear in mind that male and female genitals have more in common than popular culture leads us to believe—yup, men's genitals aren't from Mars or women's from Venus, they're both from right here on Earth.

In the womb, the genitals of both male and female fetuses are identical for the first six weeks after conception, at which point the flow of testosterone in male fetuses kicks in and starts the process of differentiation. However, male and female genitals both evolve from the same embryonic tissue, and every structure in female genitals has a corresponding structure in the male. These "homologues," or corresponding structures, will be relevant to our later discussion on the female prostate.

The vulva, or external female genitals, consists of the fleshier outer lips (the *labia majora*), the smooth, hairless inner lips (the *labia minora*), the clitoral glans, the urethral opening and the vaginal opening. The labia can vary substantially in size, color and shape. Most women find the *labia minora* sensitive to touch, and these inner lips may be a highly erogenous zone.

Another area that's sensitive for me is just inside the mouth of the vagina and the inner lips.

The Clitoris

The *labia minora* meet to form small folds at the top of the vulva, right above the clitoris. The external tip, or glans, of the clitoris is the part of a woman's genitals most sensitive to touch.

In most anatomy texts and sex manuals, you'll read about the clitoral glans and the short clitoral shaft that extends beneath the skin toward the pubic bone. Yet these descriptions are incomplete. In recent years, women's health educators and sexologists have rediscovered something that anatomists described as long ago as the seventeenth century: the clitoris is bigger than you might think. Beneath the skin, the clitoral shaft divides to form two clitoral legs (often referred to as *crura*), which run for about three inches along each side of the lower vagina. The clitoral legs correspond with the *corpus cavernosa*—the two cylinders of erectile tissue in the penis.

The clitoris is made of spongy erectile tissue, rich in blood vessels and nerve endings. During sexual arousal, increased blood flow engorges this tissue, and the entire clitoris swells and becomes firmer. When some women experience sexual pleasure from stimulation of the labia and vagina, it may be because they're indirectly stimulating the clitoral legs in the process.

An Editorial Aside

Before we discuss some other erogenous zones, we'd like to stop to sing the praises of the clitoris. Even in our post-Kinsey era, this uniquely potent source of pleasure doesn't always get the acknowledgement it deserves.

At Good Vibrations, we frequently find ourselves explaining to both men and women that the clitoris is rich in nerve endings and will transmit the sensations of a vibrator more effectively than the vagina will. Women who enjoy orgasms from clitoral stimulation still come to us asking how to have "vaginal orgasms" instead. The clitoris is too often either unknown, misunderstood or taken for granted. Yet as the only organ in nature whose exclusive purpose is to be a focal point for sexual pleasure, we think it's downright awe-inspiring.

The clitoris has been an underappreciated natural resource in the Western world due to cultural preconceptions that run roughshod over actual female experience. For centuries, the Judeo-Christian emphasis on procreation ensured that all sexual activities except penis-vagina intercourse were dismissed as "unnatural acts." The Freudian theories of female sexuality that held sway throughout the first half of the twentieth century gave the clitoris a bum rap. Freud proposed that the clitoris was an inferior, rudimentary penis and that mature women should "transfer" the source of their sexual satisfaction from the clitoris to the vagina.

In the '50s, after interviewing thousands of men and women about their sexual practices, Alfred Kinsey roundly dismissed Freud's transfer theory as a "biologic impossibility,"[2] and reported his findings that the clitoris is the primary site of sexual sensitivity in women. In the '60s, Masters and Johnson's research on human sexual response led them to state unequivocally that all women's orgasms involve the clitoris.

Although these findings have been widely popularized for over thirty years, it would appear that many women and men still don't incorporate clitoral stimulation into their sex lives. The 1994 *Sex in America* survey, promoted as being the only sex survey based on a representative sample of Americans, found that less than one-third of women always reached orgasm during sex (the type of "sex" was undefined).[3] We have to assume there's some overlap here with the fact that an estimated 50% to 75% of women require direct clitoral stimulation to reach orgasm during intercourse.[4]

All too frequently, women aren't getting the simple stimulation they need to get off. As a result, many women don't experience orgasm regularly, if at all.

It's been estimated that anywhere from 10% - 15% of women have never had an orgasm.[5] Other studies suggest that about one-third of women don't orgasm at all, one-third orgasm occasionally, and one-third orgasm fairly consistently.[6]

Given these statistics, it's no suprise that many feminists and sexologists responded to the publication of *The G Spot* with dismay and, in some cases, with derision. It has taken the better part of a century for the understanding of the clitoris as a primary site of female sexual pleasure to gain general medical and popular acceptance. If the G-spot hype revives the false ideal of a "vaginal orgasm" that is somehow more desirable than orgasm inspired by clitoral stimulation, this will deny the authenticity of many women's experience. On the other hand, it's no less unfortunate that the authentic experience of women who do enjoy G-spot stimulation is frequently denied instead.

The pendulum has swung so far away from Freud's contention that clitoral orgasm was "infantile" that I used to feel odd about much preferring to come from penetration. Learning about the G-spot was greatly validating.

If there's any moral to the story of how "standards" of female sexual response have fluctuated so widely over the centuries, it is: trust yourself, and pursue your pleasure wherever it leads you. We certainly hope that the only sexual "should" of the new millenium will be: just relax and enjoy yourself!

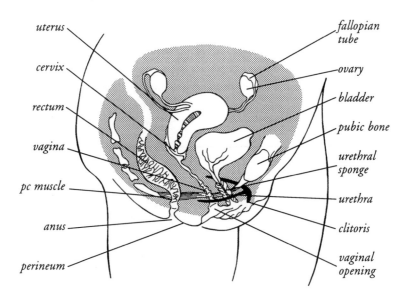

The Urethra and Urethral Sponge

The urethral opening is between the clitoris and the vaginal opening. Some women find stimulation of the area surrounding the urethral opening highly arousing; other find it unremarkable; and still others find it unpleasant. This acorn-shaped protrusion is filled with nerve endings.

The urethra is a slender tube which conducts urine out of the bladder. It's surrounded by spongy erectile tissue, containing what are known as paraurethral glands and ducts ("para" simply means "beside," or "near"). The size of this tissue and the distribution of the paraurethral glands varies from woman to woman. In their 1981 guide, *A New View of a Woman's Body*, the Federation of Feminist Health Care Centers dubbed this spongy body the "urethral sponge."

The urethral sponge swells during sexual arousal, and some women find it particularly arousing to stimulate this area, usually by pressing against it through the front wall of the vagina. Stimulation of the urethral sponge can lead to an ejaculation of fluid through the urethra. All women have a urethral sponge, but only some women report urethral ejaculations. While research has yet to determine whether female ejaculatory fluid comes from the paraurethral glands, the bladder or both, the majority of studies have demonstrated that this fluid is chemically distinct from urine.

For centuries, numerous anatomists and doctors have referred to the urethral sponge as the "female prostate," since it is structurally similar to the male prostate gland and derives from the same embryonic tissue. Recent studies have found that the female prostate produces secretions that are similar in their chemical composition to male prostatic secretions.[7] We'll address the topic of these secretions and their relationship to female ejaculate in the next chapter.

While there's some controversy over the appropriate name for this conglomerate of tissue, nerve endings, glands and ducts, no one disputes that it exists. In referring to this entity, we alternate between using the terms "urethral sponge" and "female prostate," except in our discussion of tips and techniques, where we use the popular term "G-spot."

Although the G-spot has not been anatomically identified, it seems logical to assume that it corresponds to that area of the urethral sponge that can be felt through the wall of the vagina. Some researchers are cautious about making a wholesale pronouncement that the G-spot is identical to the urethral sponge, noting that it's possible they are separate structures, or that they are related in some women but not in others.[8] However, for simplicity's sake, and because this matches our own and our customers' experience, we will be referring to them as one and the same.

At this point it's worth noting that the urethra runs parallel to the vagina, above it or closer to the front of the body. Essentially, the floor of the urethra lies next to the ceiling (or what's frequently referred to as the front wall) of the vagina. So a woman pressing into the front wall of her vagina will feel the urethral sponge. If you're wondering how a spongy area can feel like a "spot," bear in mind that a woman's urethra averages between one and a half to two inches long. We're not talking about miles of open country here.

The Vagina

The vagina is a highly muscular—and therefore highly expandable—organ lined with mucous membrane. In an unaroused state, the walls of the vagina rest against each other, but upon arousal, the walls expand outward. The vagina curves from its opening back and up toward the uterus. When we refer to the "front" or "anterior" wall of the vagina, we're referring to the wall closest to the abdomen. When we refer to the "back" wall of the vagina, we're referring to the wall closest to the spine.

If you reach just inside the vaginal opening, you'll notice that the surface of the walls feels slightly ridged and furrowed, especially along the front wall in the area where the urethral sponge protrudes. This outer third of the vagina contains more nerve endings than the inner two-thirds and can be quite responsive to touch. The inner two-thirds of the vagina are smoother, contain fewer nerve endings, and are more responsive to pressure than touch.

The vagina averages about four inches long, and curves slightly upwards toward the cervix, the entrance to the uterus. Most women find the cervix is more responsive to pressure than to touch. Some women find pressure on the cervix to be quite painful, for instance if the cervix is pummelled during intercourse. Others find it exquisitely sensitive.

Another area that's sensitive is the end of my uterus. The pressure there seems to be connected to my spine. When someone is thrusting deep and connects with me, it's much more sensitive than my G-spot.

Several of our survey respondents described an area near the cervix as being a highly erogenous zone. Upon arousal, the uterus tends to elevate, while the inner vagina expands (what's often referred to as "ballooning"), creating a sort of cul-de-sac behind the cervix. Some women find that pressure deep inside the vagina, behind the cervix, is a uniquely pleasurable sensation.

The G-spot isn't of much interest to me because there's a spot even deeper inside me that produces ecstatic orgasms. Rhythmic, slow thrusting against my "deep spot" creates a melting sensation, and I feel my orgasm growing and growing with each touch. I haven't quite been able to reproduce the sensation on my own, though I've found what works best is a double-headed dildo that I can really hold onto and move with long thrusts.

I have a spot back by my cervix that feels very good when steadily pressed on by a dildo or penis. And pulling away from this spot sends a surge of even more intense pleasure all through me—it's like a bell being struck. I call it my J-spot, after the fantasy lover I was with when I found it.

The Anus and Perineal Sponge

The anus is loaded with nerve endings, and anal stimulation can be just as arousing as genital stimulation. Between the vaginal opening and the anus lies the perineum, and between the back wall of the vagina and the rectum lies another body of spongy erectile tissue, appropriately dubbed the perineal sponge. This area is the center of numerous crisscrossing muscles of the pelvic floor. It's connected to the pudendal nerve (the primary nerve pathway for clitoral stimulation as well), and can be a highly erogenous zone. The perineal sponge probably contributes to stimulation during both vaginal and anal penetration.

It's All in How You Look at Things

Some of the female medical educators and researchers who have written about the clitoris and the urethral sponge have been inspired to propose new ways of envisioning the female genitals. Instead of subscribing to the generally accepted model in which the clitoris and its shaft are described as a miniature penis, and the urethra, vagina and perineum are all viewed as separate, unrelated bodies, they suggest instead that all these structures cohere as one functional unit that is homologous to the penis.

In her 1987 book, *Eve's Secrets*, Josephine Lowndes Sevely proposes a model of female sexual response in which the clitoris, vagina and urethra are recognized as a coordinated entity similar to the penis. Just as the entire penis—consisting of the two *corpus cavernosa*, the *corpus spongiosum* (the spongy tissue making up the glans and surrounding the urethra) and the urethra—is a unified structure, so are the female genitals. The structures that comprise the female genitals respond to sexual stimulation in concert.

In *A New View of a Woman's Body*, the authors redefine the clitoris to encompass the entire genital area, noting: "thinking of the clitoris as a functional unit, which it is, is very different from thinking of it as a collection of structures and areas as described by Masters and Johnson. Once understood and recognized, it is clear that the clitoris is an organ as complex and active as the penis."[9]

While the *New View* model, which results in cumbersome locutions such as "the pudendal nerve of the clitoris," or "the urethral sponge of the clitoris," may strike you as so much hair-splitting, the basic premise that a woman's genitals interact as one whole, rather than as a set of disconnected entities, can be a powerfully liberating one. We encourage you to keep this holistic model in mind as you read on.

Nothing New Under the Sun

There are very few true "discoveries" in the realm of human sexuality. Instead, we tend to "rediscover" anatomical and physiological information that is either ignored or denied when it doesn't fit prevailing social constructs. In this chapter, we explore Western historical writings—some of which date back over two thousand years—on the subjects of vaginal erogenous zones, the female prostate and female ejaculation. As it happens, some of the hottest "new" facts about female sexuality were common knowledge in the ancient world.

Vaginal Erogenous Zones

Celebrating the clitoris

The empirical study of sexual response is a twentieth-century discipline, and it wasn't until the '40s and '50s that doctors and sex researchers attempted to scientifically determine the sites of female sexual pleasure. In one pioneering research project by the Kinsey Institute, gynecologists studied the genital sensitivity of almost 900 women by testing the clitoris, labia, cervix and vaginal walls for responsiveness to touch.

To avoid accusations of having an overly zealous bedside manner, the doctors employed "glass, metal or cotton-tipped" probes rather than their own hands. In the project's results, published in *Sexual Behavior in the Human Female*, Kinsey reported that 98% of his subjects had clitoral sensitivity, and he became one of the first researchers to hail the clitoris as the primary site of sexual arousal in women.[10]

As only 14% of his subjects reported consciousness of vaginal touch, Kinsey concluded that the vagina was sexually unresponsive. He did note that, "most of those who did make some response had the sensitivity confined to certain points, in most cases on the upper (anterior) walls of the vagina just inside the vaginal entrance," but he suggested that the base of the clitoris was the source of this sensitivity.[11]

Of course, it's hardly surprising that gentle stroking of the vagina with the equivalent of a Q-tip went unnoticed. In fact, Kinsey had found that 90% of his subjects were responsive to vaginal pressure, but this didn't alter his opinion that the vagina was "of minimum importance in contributing to the erotic responses of the female."[12]

Unveiling the urethra

It was left to another researcher, Ernst Grafenberg, a German obstetrician and gynecologist, to more fully describe the erogenous zone that Kinsey had mentioned in passing. In a 1944 article on the cervical cap, Grafenberg and the American ob/gyn Robert L. Dickinson identified "a zone of erogenous feeling ... located along the suburethral surface of the anterior vaginal wall."[13]

In a subsequent article "The Role of Urethra in Female Orgasm, " published in 1950, Grafenberg elaborated:

An erotic zone always could be demonstrated on the anterior wall of the vagina along the course of the urethra.... Analogous to the male urethra, the female urethra also seems to be surrounded by erectile tissue like the corpora cavernosa. *In the course of sexual stimulation, the female urethra begins to enlarge and can be felt easily. It swells out greatly at the end of orgasm. The most stimulating part is located at the posterior urethra, where it arises from the neck of the bladder.*[14]

Yet Grafenberg's studies failed to generate much follow up. After all, this was the era when the clitoris was finally being scientifically verified as a "legitimate" focus of female pleasure. In a way, Grafenberg was in the wrong place at the wrong time. And perhaps he was talking about the wrong place as well. When you get right down to it, the concept of the urethra as an erogenous zone doesn't have a whole lot of sex appeal. As one feminist writer has pointed out, a self-help book entitled "The U Spot" or "The Sensuous Urethra" probably would not have had the same impact that *The G Spot* did.[15]

How the G-spot got its name

Eventually, Grafenberg's vaginal erogenous zone was destined to have its day in the sun. In the early '80s, John Perry, a sexologist and biofeed-

Beware of absolutes

Masters and Johnson published their landmark research on the physiology of orgasm in the '60s. Their work focused on the similarities between male and female sexual response. They identified the clitoris as the trigger for all female orgasm and rejected Freud's notion of the vaginal orgasm wholesale.

It's easier to recognize how outmoded assumptions have led to incomplete interpretations of human sexual behavior in the past than it is to recognize how contemporary assumptions can skew our perceptions. The research of Masters and Johnson has had a huge impact on modern-day views of sexuality, and their theories have as much credence today as Freud's did in his day. Yet Masters and Johnson's analysis was guided by their desire to determine a pattern of sexual response common to all men and women. This led them to choose their subjects and interpret physiological data somewhat selectively.

Interestingly, the only two differences Masters and Johnson recognized between male and female sexual response were that men ejaculated and women didn't; and that women were capable of multiple orgasm and men weren't. Both these assumptions have been challenged in recent years, further evidence that human sexual response is so rich, fluid and varied that it's pointless to declare any absolutes.

back practitioner, and Beverly Whipple, a registered nurse and sexologist, published studies in which they identified specific areas of vaginal sensitivity.

Think of the vagina as a clock, with twelve o'clock pointing toward the navel and six o'clock pointing toward the perineum. In one study of 47 women, Perry and Whipple found that 90% of their subjects reported twelve o'clock—in other words, the front wall of the vagina—as a highly sensitive area.[16] In further studies, Perry and Whipple had a physician or nurse examine over 400 female volunteers, all of whom identified a sensitive area in the front wall of the vagina.[17] Out of regard for the pioneering work of Ernst Grafenberg, they named this area the "Grafenberg" or "G spot."

This term has resulted in some confusion. Although the authors of *The G Spot* stated that "The G spot is probably composed of a complex network of blood vessels, the paraurethral glands and ducts, nerve endings, and the tissue surrounding the bladder neck,"[18] their accompanying references to "a spot inside the vagina," which "when properly stimulated, ... swells and leads to orgasm in many women,"[19] set off a stampede of women and men looking for a magic bean-shaped spot in the vagina.

Other researchers throughout the '80s have reported that vaginal sensitivity is common in the front wall of the vagina; however, as yet there's no consensus regarding the existence of the G-spot. In the 1988 edition of *Human Sexuality*, Masters, Johnson and Kolodny reported finding that only 10% of the women they studied had an area of sensitivity that resembled descriptions of the G-spot.[20]

Whipple and Perry suggest that some researchers may be unable to locate the spot because it doesn't swell until a woman is sexually aroused, and is therefore easily missed in a clinical setting. Furthermore, some researchers (and laypeople!) continue to seek a spot "on" the vaginal wall, rather than looking for an entity which can be felt "through" the vaginal wall.[21]

At this point, in the majority of writing on the subject, the G-spot is identified as the area of the urethral sponge that can be felt through the wall of the vagina. This urethral sponge, also referred to as the female prostate, has actually been described in anatomical literature for as many as two thousand years.

The Female Prostate

Ancient sexual texts from around the world include references to the erogenous potential of the front wall of the vagina. Indian Tantric writings mention "the sacred spot," and Chinese Taoist texts reveal how to best stimulate "the black pearl."[22] In the Western World, the term

"female prostate" crops up in writings dating back to the time of
Aristotle. Galen, the second century Greek physician whose theories
influenced medicine up until the Renaissance, made references to both
the female prostate gland and female prostatic fluid.

Regnier De Graaf, a Dutch anatomist of the seventeenth century,
published exceptionally accurate descriptions of the male and female
genitals. In his *New Treatise Concerning the Generative Organs of Women*,
he offered probably the first scientific description of women's urethral
glands, referring to them as the female prostate.

Numerous gynecologists and urologists have studied the female urethral glands and ducts throughout the past century. In the 1880s,
Alexander Skene identified two ducts just inside the urethral opening,
which have gone by the name of "Skene's glands" ever since. Doctors in
the 1940s and '50s determined that these glands were more extensive
than Skene had realized and many compared them to the male prostate.
Although most of these medical experts considered the female prostate
to be a vestigial structure, they also noted that the female urethral
glands secreted fluid comparable to male prostatic fluid and contained
erectile tissue comparable to the *corpus spongiosum* in the penis.

Much of this historical overview was compiled by Josephine
Lowndes Sevely and J.W. Bennett in a 1978 article for the *Journal of
Sex Research* entitled "Concerning Female Ejaculation and the Female
Prostate." This article served as inspiration for the authors of *The G
Spot*, who, in turn, have inspired numerous studies on the scope and
function of female urethral glands.

Several recent studies have confirmed parallels between the structure, secretions and enzymes of the male prostate and the female urethral glands. While some researchers draw the line at declaring the two
entities to be homologous, many others feel that the term "female
prostate" is completely appropriate.[23]

After all, both male and female prostates derive from the same
embryonic tissue. They're both made up of glands and ducts, and both
structures wrap around the urethra. Both swell when they are stimulated, and both produce secretions.

There are certain notable differences. The female prostate doesn't
develop the way the male prostate does because it isn't stimulated by
male hormones (androgens). Therefore, it's smaller than that of the

male, and less consistent in size, shape and location. Researchers have found that the extent of female prostatic tissue, its development and the distribution of glands can vary substantially, possibly influenced by hormonal factors such as a woman's age and whether or not she's given birth.

Sexual stimulation of the urethral sponge has clearly been linked with the phenomenon of ejaculation. While it's certain that some women ejaculate fluid through the urethra, both upon sexual arousal and at orgasm, the precise composition of this fluid is still being debated. One thing's for sure: there's a long and compelling body of literature devoted to the topic of female ejaculation.

Female Fluids

A juicy history lesson

Throughout history, the concept of female ejaculation has been recognized, both as folk knowledge and in anatomical texts. Yet this knowledge has been suppressed and dismissed by the medical establishment over the past three centuries, to reemerge only quite recently.

From the time of Hippocrates, the fifth-century B.C. "Father of Medicine," up until the eighteenth-century Enlightenment, it was widely believed that the mingled sexual fluids of both men and women were necessary for conception. The second-century physician Galen explicitly distinguished between female "seed"—which he believed contributed to conception—and female prostatic fluid—which he believed contributed to sexual pleasure:

... the fluid in her prostate is unconcocted and thin. This contributes nothing to the generation of offspring. Properly, then, it is poured outside when it has done its service....This liquid not only stimulates the sexual act but also is able to give pleasure and moisten the passageway as it escapes. It manifestly flows from women as they experience the greatest pleasure in coitus. [24]

In the seventeenth century, the Dutch anatomist Regnier De Graaf wrote at length about the female prostate and its erotic potential, noting that female prostatic fluid "rushes out with impetus," frequently

Ejaculation around the world

The notion that both women and men ejaculate fluids during sexual pleasure and orgasm is by no means restricted to the Western world. It's written in the *Kama Sutra of Vatsyayana* that "the semen of women continues to fall from the beginning of the sexual union to its end,"[25] and Japanese erotic art frequently depicts secretions flowing out of women.[26]

The sixteenth-century Arabic manual, *The Perfumed Garden*, instructs male readers to engage in "playful frolics" with women before intercourse to guarantee mutual pleasure, observing "acting thus, the two ejaculations occur simultaneously, and enjoyment is complete for both."[27] Anthropological reports ranging from the South Pacific to Africa to the American West positively swim in accounts of female ejaculation.[28]

In the modern era, these references have been dismissed as cases of mistaken identity. It's assumed that descriptions of female ejaculation in ancient sex manuals and erotica derive from poetic license in describing vaginal secretions. Western anthropologists frequently dismissed their subjects' reports of ejaculation as instances of urination during sex, as did physicians and other health professionals.

The conviction that, despite all evidence to the contrary, women can't possibly be ejaculating continues up to the present day, and has led to some elaborate counter-arguments. One sexologist deriding the theories put forth in *The G Spot* argued that so-called ejaculate was possibly "left-over bath water which is expelled with powerful orgasmic uterine contractions."[29] Talk about throwing the baby of authentic female experience out with the bath water!

inspired by "frisky fingers." He offered this lively description of female ejaculate:

The function of the "prostate" is to generate a juice which makes women more libidinous with its pungency and saltiness and lubricates their sexual parts in agreeable fashion during coitus.... Here too it should be noted that the discharge from the female "prostatae" causes as much pleasure as does that from the male "prostatae." [30]

Historians have pointed out that before the eighteenth century men and women were widely believed to be equally enthusiastic about sex and it was expected that both would orgasm and ejaculate.[31] The authors of *The G Spot* and *Eve's Secrets* theorize that once the microscope came into common use, and scientists could corroborate that female fluids didn't contain sperm and therefore didn't contribute to conception, they dropped the subject of female ejaculation from medical literature. It was as if the phenomenon had never existed.[32]

However, the subject lived on in popular writings. Victorian erotica is filled with references to women and men "spending" their fluids together. That classic of Victorian "voluptuous reading," *The Pearl*, drips with references to women opening the "floodgates of love's reservoir" to release "streams of pearly essence."

Twentieth-century views

Despite these ongoing anecdotal reports, female ejaculation disappeared from medical discourse until Grafenberg published his research on the urethra as an erogenous zone—a topic that had been ignored in the three centuries since De Graaf. He described his findings with details that are immediately familiar to anyone who's experienced female ejaculation:

This convulsory expulsion of fluids occurs always at the acme of the orgasm and simultaneously with it. If there is the opportunity to observe the orgasm of such women, one can see that large quantities of a clear transparent fluid are expelled not from the vulva, but out of the urethra in gushes. At first I thought that the bladder sphincter had become defective by the intensity of the orgasm. Involuntary expulsion of urine is reported in sex literature. In the cases observed by us, the fluid was examined and it had no urinary character. I am inclined to believe that "urine" reported to be expelled during female orgasm is not urine, but only secretions of the intraurethral glands correlated with the erotogenic zone along the urethra in the anterior vaginal wall. Moreover, the profuse secretions coming out with the orgasm have no lubricating significance, otherwise they would be produced at the beginning of intercourse and not at the peak of orgasm.[33]

Grafenberg's research was shunted aside for several decades, and the leading sexologists of the second half of the century thoroughly pooh-poohed the idea that women expelled any fluid but urine from the urethra. While well aware of the anecdotal evidence and clinical descriptions of female ejaculation, Kinsey dismissed the phenomenon, suggesting that these reports were based on incidences in which women with strong pelvic muscles forcefully ejected vaginal lubrication.[34]

Masters and Johnson rejected the notion of female ejaculation as "erroneous," and suggested that women who claimed such a response were probably suffering from urinary stress incontinence. Even after the publication of *The G Spot*, they continued to be skeptical, and Masters has only recently been quoted as saying he now believes ejaculation can occur in the "rare female."[35]

However, as we'll discuss in "All About Ejaculation" (p. 28), new research is providing much greater insight into female ejaculation.

Exploration

Communication

Before you dive into some hands-on research, it's a good idea to review your expectations. Are you hot on the trail of a "no-hands" orgasm? Are you worried that everybody else on the block is ejaculating but you? Are you determined to locate a magical ecstasy button that will make your girlfriend come like a rocket? Well, stop right there!

We can't repeat this often enough: A goal-oriented approach is more likely to diminish your enjoyment than to enhance your sex life. Your best bet is to put aside all expectations and to explore your body for the simple fun of it. The fact that you're willing to investigate new forms of stimulation guarantees that you'll learn something new about your sexual responses—and when it comes to sex, knowledge isn't just power, it's pleasure.

Talking about the G-spot

If you're a woman who has never experienced G-spot stimulation, you may prefer to make some expeditions on your own before you bring a partner along. Masturbation is the ideal medium for sexual experimentation, and you can easily incorporate some of the suggestions below into solo sex.

Even if you're familiar with hitting the spot, it may be difficult for you to reach the G-spot yourself. If you have a partner, consider asking him or her for assistance. It's often less threatening to bring up sexual requests outside of a sexual setting, for instance: "I just read a book about the G-spot—would you like to find out what mine feels like sometime?"

Or you may find it perfectly natural to invite your partner to tour your vaginal geography during a playful sexual encounter. Whichever route you take, make sure to be specific in your requests, explicit with feedback as to what kind of stimulation feels good and willing to try a variety of strokes and positions. Sexual techniques aren't "one-size-fits-all," and the only way to identify your personal preferences is to practice, practice, practice!

If you're interested in finding out whether your partner enjoys G-spot stimulation, make sure you're clear about your own motivation before you raise the subject. Are you hoping she'll orgasm during intercourse, or have some kind of new, "better" orgasm? Are you hoping to recreate the sexual scenario you shared with a different partner? If you have your own agenda about the kind of responses she "could" or "should" be having, you'll wind up sending out signals that are anything but arousing.

You and your partner will have a better time if you take a flexible, open-minded approach to your explorations. Every woman is different in her response to G-spot stimulation, and each individual's responses may fluctuate over the course of a month, a year or a lifetime. What's pleasurable today may be less so tomorrow, and vice versa. Spare yourselves the pressures of performance anxiety, and focus on having a good time.

Talking about ejaculation

Many women have been embarrassed by ejaculating, especially if they or their partner have mistaken the ejaculate for urine. Fortunately, more women and men have become familiar with the phenomenon of female ejaculation in recent years, so these cases of mistaken identity are fewer and farther between. If you have a partner who remains unconvinced that female ejaculation truly is distinct from urine, you can show him or her this book. If your partner still remains disturbed by your ejaculation, try to identify his or her specific concerns: Does she think ejaculation is something only men do? Does he wonder what other "secret" talents you might be keeping under wraps?

Most likely, a partner who feels a bit squeamish about female ejaculation just needs some time to get used to the idea and the sensation. The more familiar with your sexual responses and comfortable with your own bodily fluids you are, the better equipped you'll be to normalize the subject. And there are practical considerations worth discussing. For instance, nobody likes sleeping on a soggy mattress. In the interests of full disclosure, you might tell a new partner: "Sometimes I ejaculate when I'm really aroused, so I'd prefer to keep a towel on the bed just in case."

In the vast majority of cases, your partner will be intrigued and excited by your ejaculation. The landscape of female pleasure has been *terra incognita* for so long that a visible and dramatic expression of sexual pleasure is highly arousing to lovers of women.

When I've been with women who ejaculate, their orgasm is usually very intense ... and I sure do like the shower!

The first time I ejaculated, I didn't know what was happening. What felt like "water" just ran out of me and down my thighs. It was warm, and my partner went nuts with excitement.

How to Hit the Spot

By now you're probably ready to get cracking and find out what the G-spot feels like. Here are a few helpful hints to keep in mind.

Everyone's different
You or your partner may find you love G-spot stimulation. You may think it's a nice enhancement, but hardly mind-blowing. You may not feel much of anything. Or you may find it downright uncomfortable. For one thing, everybody has unique sexual responses, and just as no two women will respond to nipple stimulation in exactly the same way, no two women will respond to G-spot stimulation in exactly the same way. For another thing, the size and development of the urethral sponge can vary from woman to woman, so for you the G-spot may be literally no big deal.

The G-spot is a little bit of heaven located just the other side of the pubic bone on the upper wall of the vagina ... yummmm.

G-spot stimulation doesn't really do too much for me. It's an interesting sensation, but I don't get off on it. One of my lovers finds it very uncomfortable, another found it very stimulating.

Set the stage

It's easier to find the G-spot if you're already aroused, as the urethral sponge will have begun to swell and be more prominent. You're also more likely to enjoy the sensations of G-spot stimulation if you're excited to begin with.

Stimulating my G-spot is a powerful sensation, if I am already aroused. If I'm not aroused already, G-spot stimulation doesn't seem to get me there.

I have to feel the need for it in order for it to be pleasurable. If I'm touched there without wanting it, the sensation is annoying and uncomfortable.

When you first stimulate the G-spot, you'll probably feel an urge to urinate. After a few seconds, this sensation should subside. If it would make you more comfortable to know that your bladder is empty, try urinating before you embark on your explorations. The "oh no, I'm gonna pee!" sensation is a natural result of pressure against your urethra. With experience, you may come to reinterpret this sensation as purely pleasurable.

G-spot stimulation can initially feel unpleasant (due to a desire to urinate), but then the sensations become much more intense, deep and full-bodied than those from clitoral stimulation.

First contact with my G-spot usually results in a quick jolt of pleasure, then continues as a long, comfortably energetic feeling.

Location, location, location

You may or may not be able to reach the front wall of your vagina with your own fingers, especially if you're lying on your back. Some women report that they can reach the G-spot when lying on their backs as long as their knees are pressed up against their chests.

Usually I'm on my back, propped up against pillows. I need my legs drawn up so my knees and thighs are wide. Partly this just feels damn good, and partly this makes it possible for me to stroke my own cervix and G-spot.

You'll probably find it easier to try squatting, lying on your stomach, or propping yourself on your hands and knees. Reach your fingers an inch or two in from the vaginal opening, and crook them toward the front wall of the vagina in a "come hither" motion.

The G-spot is responsive to pressure, but not to light touch. If you brush lightly around the inside of the vagina, you'll probably not feel anything. Instead, press firmly into the vaginal wall. Remember, the G-spot isn't *on* the vaginal wall; it's felt *through* the vaginal wall.

As you explore the vaginal wall from the pubic bone up toward the cervix, you should feel a slightly ridged area that begins to swell. You may find it helpful to take your other hand and press down on the outside of your belly just above the pubic hair line—sometimes you can feel the G-spot area swelling between your two hands. Here's how some of our survey respondents describe the G-spot:

To me the G-spot feels just like it's described in various texts: a spongy circle about the size of an almond. Mine is located just in front of my cervix, in the top of the vaginal wall. I felt for it with my middle finger once when I was masturbating and was rather surprised to find it so easily.

The G-spot feels like a small cushion nestled up against my pubic bone—the texture of the skin there seems different, lightly ridged as opposed to the super-smooth skin around it.

My G-spot is about half a finger-joint from the entrance to the vagina. It feels like a low mound with the texture of soft pumice, sort of like a ripe strawberry.

Let your partner's fingers do the walking

Many women find it easiest to locate the G-spot with the help of a friend. Perhaps you can't quite reach the G-spot, or you can't comfortably sustain pressure on it with your own fingers. This is why some women only become aware of the G-spot with the help of a partner.

I can't tell you how to get there, but I sure know when you're there!

I discovered the spot rather clinically when a boyfriend who was taking a sexuality class guided me in looking for it.

The following words are addressed to nimble-fingered partners everywhere. If you're interested in stimulating your partner's G-spot, you're likely to have the greatest success by exploring the front wall of her vagina with your fingers.

I haven't had much success hitting the G-spot with anything but fingers. Most toys don't have the right curve. I've had the best results on my back and on my stomach with a partner's fingers—he uses them well.

For G-spot stimulation, I need to be on my back, knees up, back rounded. It's very hard to reach the spot myself; I need a partner with agile fingers.

Start with your partner lying on her stomach, legs apart, with her hips slightly raised. Insert your index and/or middle fingers, palm down, and press against the front wall of her vagina in the area behind the pubic bone. Alternately, you can launch your explorations with your partner on her back, knees up, while you crook your fingers up toward her navel. Experiment with circling, rocking and massaging motions, but keep your touch firm and consistent. Ask your partner for feedback. With time and practice, you'll both learn what does the trick.

I find steady pressure against the G-spot most pleasurable. Manipulation or rubbing is irritating and makes me feel as if I have to urinate. Constant pressure with a penis (from behind), fingers or a curved dildo is best.

I can tell when I've hit the spot because my partner makes a tensing motion inside her vagina.

Once you've located the G-spot, you can try hooking your fingers behind the pubic bone and rhythmically pressing into the area; your thumb and the palm of your hand will be in position to stimulate her clitoris at the same time.

I use two fingers to penetrate my lover and stroke the G-spot with fairly strong but short movements until she ejaculates.

I get the best stimulation from one or two fingers massaging slowly and forcefully.

Some women find that one or two fingers don't provide sufficient stimulation of the G-spot and that they have to be "filled up" before they become aware of it. Every woman has a different comfort zone regarding penetration, and personal preferences range from a-pinky-at-most to king-sized-is-best. The vagina is highly muscular and expandable; with sufficient time, arousal and lubricant, many women can accommodate an entire hand in the vagina. "Fisting" is the term used for penetrating a partner with your hand.

If you or your partner enjoy vaginal fisting, you may discover that this is one sure-fire way to enhance awareness of all the vaginal hot spots. As Annie Sprinkle cheerily comments in her video *Sluts and Goddesses*, "if you really can't locate your Goddess-spot, try getting fist-fucked and you can't miss it!"

I've discovered that while being fisted my sensitivity level goes up so dramatically that any pressure anywhere inside the vagina feels incredibly erotic and stimulating, but that during penetration with a dildo or fingers, that intense sensation is not there. I think the pressure of fisting is stimulating the G-spot.

Positions

If you find G-spot stimulation arousing, you may want to incorporate it into intercourse. Certain intercourse positions lend themselves best to hitting the spot. Woman-on-top and rear entry, with the woman either on her stomach or on her side, are popular intercourse positions. In fact, Grafenberg speculated that the G-spot links us to our primate past. Since nearly all mammals have rear-entry intercourse, there would be an evolutionary benefit to females deriving particular pleasure from this position.[36]

Most efficient lately has been entry from behind. In general, I need to have a lot of freedom of hip and body movement. I also like to arch my back.

The first time I had rear-entry intercourse, the depth achieved was greater than ever before, and I became out of control when my G-spot was stimulated. I wasn't sure what it was at the time.

Even when masturbating, I have to be face down and spread really wide in order to stimulate my G-spot.

Face-to-face positions don't tend to work very well, unless the penis or dildo has a distinct curve or unless the woman has her legs over her partner's shoulders. Some couples experiment with kneeling positions or partial insertion, so that the head of the penis or dildo is rubbing against the front wall of the vagina.

If I pull out most of the way, the ridge of my penis will stroke her G-spot, so I can have repeated shallow penetrations. Usually she's on her back with her legs raised up.

T-shapes are the best positions! On the table, the edge of the bed, or with my partner sitting up on his heels while I have a pillow under my butt. I need hard, regular thrusting and firm pressure.

But everybody's anatomy is individual, and it's up to you to figure out the angles that work best for you.

During partner sex, we found that if my lover lay on her back it was easiest to find her G-spot since it was really angled upwards and sort of difficult to get to if she was on her hands and knees or if we were standing up face to face.

Interestingly, the sixteenth-century Arabic sex manual, *The Perfumed Garden*, describes an intercourse position named "pounding the spot," which is reputed by "universal consent" to give the most satisfaction to women. In this position, "the man sits down and stretches out his legs, and the woman sits on his thighs and crosses her legs behind his back....She then puts her arms round his neck, and he puts his round her waist and raises and lowers her on his member, in which movement she assists."[37] Sounds like a good way to hit the G-spot!

You may find that intercourse is not your preferred approach to G-spot stimulation. Perhaps the movement of thrusting doesn't provide sufficiently consistent pressure on the area, or perhaps you and your partner can't quite get into the right position.

During intercourse, it's a little difficult to focus on just one spot inside.

Doggie style tends to hit the G-spot best, but I'm less aware of the G-spot during intercourse. There's too much other stimulation going on (kissing, hands massaging, bodies rubbing). If I'm determined to hit the G-spot, manual stimulation by a partner is best. No distractions.

Or you may find that G-spot stimulation greatly enhances intercourse.

The thing that is very cool is that intercourse is a whole new ball game after I have had a number of G-spot induced orgasms. I come by having intercourse when I am that aroused. The position that I come in the easiest at that time is with me on top—the stimulation is the best for me in that position.

It's worth noting that you may be unable to feel your G-spot if you're wearing a diaphragm—depending on fit and your personal anatomy, the diaphragm can block the front wall of the vagina. Again depending on fit and your personal anatomy, a cervical cap may be more likely to leave all your erogenous zones unimpeded.[38]

An abundance of pleasure

We've already mentioned that you're more likely to enjoy G-spot stimulation when you're aroused. With sexual arousal, a myriad of sensations that might otherwise be uncomfortable are transformed into exciting stimuli. It stands to reason that prodding around your urethra is unlikely to feel particularly good unless you're warmed up to begin with.

Many women begin their stimulation of the G-spot by stimulating the clitoris, labia and urethral opening. You may be surprised to discover what an erogenous zone the area around the urethral opening can be (or you may find stimulation of the urethral opening irritating under all circumstances). Once your erectile tissue is congested, external stimulation can indirectly stimulate the G-spot. This is one reason oral sex can be such a great G-spot enhancer.

It seems to me that if I go down on my lover before I play with her G-spot, the spot is much larger (more swollen) and less uncomfortably sensitive than without oral sex.

When my partner is going down on me and inserts a finger, palm up, into my vagina, and curls the finger up and back slightly, that seems to be the most effective way of hitting the spot.

Given that arousal amplifies the sensation of G-spot stimulation, it should come as no surprise that women who have multiple orgasms sometimes report that they enjoy G-spot stimulation best after having had one or two orgasms. Once the entire genital region is engorged and sensitive from orgasm, it can be easier to tune in to the "deeper" regions of erectile tissue.

G-spot stimulation is particularly pleasurable if I reach the spot while I'm already climaxing. It brings me through to another height, and I can keep going quite a bit longer with the orgasm.

Some women report that G-spot stimulation can result in unique sensations or orgasms that they distinguish from orgasms triggered by clitoral stimulation. Orgasms involving G-spot stimulation are frequently described as being more diffuse and less electric than those primarily triggered by clitoral stimulation. Sexual sensations are intensely subjective, and we certainly would never tell you you "ought" to feel any particular way from any particular stimulation, but you may find that descriptions such as these correspond with your own experience.

When someone is stimulating it for me, it is a specific spot, but what I feel isn't spot-specific in the same way—the sensation spreads out.

It feels different from straight penetration, as if different nerve endings are being stimulated. It's almost as if it's a warm, gushy feeling, rather than an intense one.

Rock Around the Clock

One of the most common ways to steer women toward the G-spot is to tell them to envision the vaginal barrel as a clockface and to press against the area of "twelve o'clock" in the vaginal wall. But there's no reason to limit your excursions to high-noon territory. Take the time to explore every surface of your vagina in order to identify any "hot spots" of your own.

In John Perry and Beverly Whipple's study of vaginal sensitivity, 90% of their subjects reported twelve o'clock to be highly sensitive. However, runners-up included eleven o'clock (57%) and one o'clock (47%), while four o'clock (30%) and eight o'clock (37%) also got honorable mentions.[39]

Presumably, there's a range of possible pleasurable sites in the front wall of the vagina, depending on the location of each woman's urethral sponge. Other women find the back wall of the vagina sensitive (four o'clock through eight o'clock), especially just inside the vaginal opening, as pressing into this wall will stimulate the perineal sponge.

All About Ejaculation

The majority of our survey respondents who enjoyed G-spot stimulation also reported experiences of ejaculating fluids from the urethra. These two phenomena are commonly linked in many people's minds, since they both burst into popular consciousness with the publication of *The G Spot*, yet they certainly can be separate occurrences.

In fact, some women ejaculate in response to G-spot stimulation, some women enjoy G-spot stimulation but never ejaculate, and some women ejaculate in response to clitoral stimulation. Some women ejaculate on arousal, and some women ejaculate upon orgasm. Ejaculation and orgasm are separate physiological events for both women and men.

Both times I ejaculated, it was caused by hard, direct pressure, in a rhythm, against the G-spot, and it was separate from orgasm.

I ejaculate during orgasm, though sometimes it's tough to say what is orgasm and what isn't (I have multiples of varying intensity). I do not ejaculate with all orgasms.

In fact, one clinical study of 27 women found that all the subjects identified a sensitive site corresponding to the G-spot area, which palpably swelled upon stimulation. However, only ten of these women ejaculated in response to G-spot stimulation, and there was a substantial range of responses among these ten women. Some ejaculated with as little as two minutes of stimulation, others with fifteen minutes. Only three of the women reported orgasm accompanying ejaculation.[40]

While there are no hard and fast rules when it comes to the phenomenon of female ejaculation, there are certain common questions and reliable observations. We'll address these "Ejaculation FAQs" next.

What stimulates ejaculation?

It appears that ejaculation is caused by stimulation of the urethral sponge. Upon stimulation, the tissue of the urethral sponge fills with blood and the paraurethral glands fill with fluid. Some women report that they can feel the glands and ducts of the urethral sponge filling with fluid.

Sometimes I can feel the ejaculate being pumped up inside me before I come. Also, sometimes when I don't ejaculate I have to "milk" the come out of me, or the pressure bothers me.

Researchers have demonstrated that the urethral glands in women secrete fluids comparable to prostatic fluids in men. Some researchers conclude that female ejaculate consists of these prostatic fluids; others theorize that it may also contain a chemically-altered form of urine. In any event, this fluid either seeps, flows or spurts out of the urethra during ejaculation.

• *Get in shape*

Certain contributing factors crop up repeatedly in women's reports of ejaculation, and good pelvic muscle tone is foremost among these. At least one study has shown that ejaculation is definitely more likely in occur in women with well-toned pubococcygeus (PC) muscles[41]—the group of muscles that supports the pelvic floor and surrounds the genital organs in both men and women. Anecdotal reports confirm that voluntary control of the PC muscle leads to greater awareness of the G-spot and the entire vaginal barrel, as well as enhancing the ability to ejaculate. For more information on identifying and exercising PC muscles, see p. 41 below.

Many women comment that right before they ejaculate, they feel compelled to bear down with their vaginal muscles—it feels as if the outer third of the vagina is pushing out, rather than contracting. In fact, some women can't ejaculate with a penis or dildo inside the vagina, as the force of the bearing-down movement ejects whatever's inside them. Others enjoy having something in the vagina as a focal point and as a G-spot stimulator.

With a partner, just about everything works to make me ejaculate except cunnilingus—I have to have enough penetration and something I can squeeze hard on. Lately, I have found it possible to ejaculate even after the stimulus is removed ("Oh, no! Sorry! I tried not to soak your couch!").

A well-toned muscle is one that you can contract *and* relax with ease. You may find that the ability to relax and just "let it flow" inspires ejaculation.

Once orgasm started, I kept up the stimulation, waiting for that "I'm gonna pee!" sensation—and what a turn-on to feel that hot fluid gush over my hand! It was a combination of being willing to "let go" more and being able to relax in a certain way and just let things happen.

Men employ the PC muscle when learning to control ejaculation or to practice techniques of multiple orgasm. It stands to reason that the muscle supporting and surrounding the urethra and vagina would play a role in female ejaculation as well.

• *More is more*

Usually it takes more than one type of stimulation to inspire ejaculation. We tend to assume that ejaculation is caused exclusively by internal stimulation of the G-spot, but this isn't necessarily the case. In fact, in Beverly Whipple's first published report analyzing ejaculatory fluid, the subject also ejaculated as a result of oral sex.[42] Most women report that they combine clitoral stimulation with G-spot stimulation to ejaculate, and many ejaculate solely from external stimulation.

I can't ejaculate without combined clitoral and G-spot stimulation. It's like my clit primes my cervix and G-spot, and my cervix feeds into my G-spot. In a way it's kind of an arousal cascade (no pun intended!)

The first time I ejaculated, my lover and I were at the ballet and she was stimulating my clit with her fingers. The thrill of watching the ballet, trying to keep quiet, and trying not to let anyone in the rows around us see me squirm made me come with a surge I had never felt before.

Basically, any type of stimulation that's liable to arouse the urethral sponge can lead to ejaculation. And since the clitoris, urethra and vagina are all quite close together, it's unlikely you could ever completely isolate one from the others, even if you wanted to.

I put pressure on my G-spot from the outside, by holding a vibrator against the opening of my urethra, just under my clit. This makes for a great blend of stimulation, and I nearly always ejaculate as a result.

• *Prime the pump*

Just as some women enjoy G-spot stimulation best after they've already had an orgasm or two, you may find it easier to ejaculate if you've already "primed the pump" by having an orgasm. All the erectile tissue of your genitals will be swollen and more sensitive to stimulation.

I don't always ejaculate when I orgasm, but I tend to ejaculate after I have had a few orgasms. This is always prompted with G-spot stimulation. There seems to be even more fluid if I have had a clitoral orgasm first and then some G-spot orgasms.

The first time I experienced female ejaculation was years ago after being stimulated orally by my lover. He kept stimulating me after I reached my "usual" orgasm, and it was such a powerful sense of building tension, it kind of scared me. I gasped out that I was going to pee and then I felt this fluid leaving me involuntarily.

I've ejaculated twice that I know of, using my Hitachi Wand vibrator with an insertable attachment. Both times I'd been making love for a good hour, with my lover and my Wand and probably a butt plug, and I was on my second or third orgasm.

If you're not someone who experiences multiple orgasms, you may simply require an extended arousal period in order to ejaculate.

Excruciatingly slow, steady build-up of arousal has always preceded my ejaculation.

How many women ejaculate?

It's possible that female ejaculation was underreported for many years, due to general ignorance and to the fact that some women ejaculate small amounts of fluid that are easily mistaken for vaginal secretions. Conversely, it's possible that ejaculation has become somewhat over-reported in recent years, and that some women may now mistake vaginal secretions for urethral ejaculations. After all, the urethral and vaginal openings are quite close together, and in the heat of the moment, it's easy to lose sight of which end is up.

There simply are no definitive figures as to what percent of women regularly ejaculate. Sex surveying is a notoriously inexact science. It's vulnerable to the unconscious biases of researchers, which can affect the questions they ask and how they ask them. Furthermore, surveys usually rely on a self-selecting pool of volunteers, which can skew the results.

We're perfectly willing to quote a few statistics, but please bear in mind that women who ejaculate are more likely to be inspired to fill out a survey about ejaculation than those who don't. Certainly far more of the respondents to our informal survey fell into the "thanks for asking about one of my favorite things" camp than the "I don't know what all the fuss is about" camp.

The authors of *The G Spot* report that when they first began asking audiences at speaking engagements how many had personally experienced female ejaculation, about 10% responded. Over time, perhaps with increased popular awareness of the topic, responses rose to 40%.[43]

One survey polling 233 subjects drawn from women's and student's groups in four cities found that 54% of respondents reported experience with "an orgasmic expulsion of fluid," though only 14% experienced this expulsion with most or all orgasms.[44]

In another extensive survey of 1245 professional women from the US and Canada, 39.5% of the respondents reported ejaculation at orgasm, while 69% of the 800 women who requested a questionnaire from Beverly Whipple reported an expulsion of fluid at orgasm.[45]

So there you have it. It's been scientifically proven that anywhere from 10% to 69% of women are ejaculators! Obviously, this is a huge range, and probably the only logical conclusion to draw is that it's perfectly natural to ejaculate and it's perfectly natural not to.

What's it made of?

The misconception that female ejaculators are actually urinating during sex has caused a great deal of unnecessary suffering. The authors of *The G Spot* suggest that some women who rarely or never orgasm may have learned to inhibit their orgasms out of fear of ejaculating. Before the phenomenon of female ejaculation was republicized in the '80s, many ejaculating women were convinced they were "wetting the bed" and underwent treatments for incontinence. Even today, many women who ejaculate spend at least some time with their noses in the sheets, checking whether the fluid smells or tastes like urine. Our survey respondents were eager to describe their anecdotal evidence of the difference between female ejaculate and urine.

It was clear and sweet and there was a lot more of it than any man's ejaculate.

The stuff smells fantastic. Very subtle when it's fresh. Once I caught some in a jar, and when I smelled it a few days later, it was musky like perfume.

I recently started experiencing a gush of clear fluid with orgasm. It wets the bed, but doesn't stain.

Sex researchers have only recently begun to tackle the challenge of identifying the source and the chemical composition of female ejaculate. There have been fewer than ten clinical studies of female ejaculate, and these studies have involved very small groups of women (between one and eleven). In other words, the ejaculate of fewer than 60 women has been analyzed since 1981. To date, the results aren't conclusive, but they are intriguing.

In the majority of the studies, researchers found significant chemical differences between the ejaculate and urine of subjects. In some instances, female ejaculate was found to contain higher levels of prostatic acid phosphatase (or PAP), formerly thought to be exclusive to male prostatic secretions, as well as higher levels of glucose or fructose, also distinctive to prostatic fluid. Ejaculate was also found to contain significantly lower levels of urea and creatinine, the primary components of urine. Several researchers therefore concluded that female ejaculate consists of secretions from the female prostate and is homologous to male prostatic fluid.[46]

In a recent research project for San Francisco's Institute for Advanced Study of Human Sexuality, Dr. Gary Schubach set up an experiment attempting to determine whether the source of female ejaculate is the bladder or the urethral glands. His subjects were seven women who reported ejaculating regularly during sexual arousal. He catheterized these women in order to isolate the bladder from the urethra and drained fluid from their bladders while they stimulated themselves to arousal and orgasm.

The fluid drained from his subjects' bladders during sexual arousal and orgasm was significantly different from urine samples collected prior to arousal, having a reduced concentration of urea and creatinine. Schubach concluded, "the clear inference is that the expelled fluid is an altered form of urine and that there is a process that goes on during sensual/sexual stimulation and excitement that changes the chemical composition of urine."[47] During Schubach's experiment, a milky-white, mucous-like fluid seeped from the urethra around the catheter tube in four of the subjects. There weren't sufficient quantities of this fluid to analyze, but Schubach speculated that the thicker fluid was an emission from the urethral glands.

If female ejaculate is sort of like a cocktail, combining an altered form of urine and prostatic fluids, this could explain the conflicting results of previous studies. "In the cases where prostatic fluid components were discovered, a urethral expulsion may have also taken place. In other instances, where there was just fluid with lowered amounts of urea and creatinine, an expulsion from the bladder only may have been involved."[48]

Further research is required to definitively identify the nature of female ejaculate. Yet as far as we're concerned, it doesn't really matter what it's made of or where it comes from: if it feels good, let the fluids fly. After all, clinical analyses pale in comparison to evocative, firsthand descriptions such as this one:

When my lover ejaculates, the texture of the liquid over her G-spot and in her vagina as a whole changes from a silky feel to something more like water—the liquid floods and gushes. It's a sharp, exciting contrast. The taste also changes—it becomes salty, tart, almost savory.

How much fluid is ejaculated?

Here's another aspect of female ejaculation that's almost impossible to quantify reliably. While many people can rattle off the factoid that the average male ejaculate is a teaspoon or two in volume, there's no such unananimity when it comes to women coming.

We've read documented observations of ejaculatory expulsions ranging in volume from a quarter teaspoon to a quarter cup to almost a quart![49] The authors of *The G Spot* suggest that anecdotal reports of women ejaculating pints of fluid may be simply a matter of perception. After all, many women would be surprised to hear that they're only contending with an average of four tablespoons of menstrual blood every month. When it's coming out of your body, a little fluid can make a big impression.

Volume of ejaculate can vary from woman to woman and from experience to experience. There's also a wide range in women's ejaculatory styles. Just as few men deliver porn star ejaculations, sending a geyser of semen exploding across the room, few women actually hose down the walls. Some women emit a light flow of fluid, while others squirt more forcefully.

The first time I ejaculated, it wasn't intense, but it was sudden, and it was flowing rather than coming out in a hard stream.

The only experience I had with female ejaculation happened one time with a partner using his fingers to rub the front wall of my vagina. At orgasm, extra fluid seeped from the vagina. It didn't shoot out across the room as I've heard others describe, but it was definitely something special.

Probably all women emit prostatic secretions, but that doesn't mean that all women emit them in sufficient abundance to be noticeable. The long and short of it is that some women need to keep towels next to the bed and others don't. This diversity of experience certainly doesn't mean that some women are "better" ejaculators than others. The last thing we need is to transform female ejaculation into the latest track and field event of the sexual Olympics, with medals awarded for height and volume.

Of course, there is one arena in which female ejaculation *is* something of a performance-art event. "Squirting" or "gushing" has become a popular speciality genre in adult video. Until the early '90s, depictions of female ejaculation were few and far between in adult video, and largely confined to independent or educational films.

Mainstream porn producers adhere to certain unwritten, yet rigid, industry conventions, steering clear of depicting any activities which might be deemed legally "obscene." Since depicting urination is legally problematic, for many years video producers didn't want to risk depicting female ejaculation, if they even knew there was a difference between urination and ejaculation. In recent years, increased awareness of the phenomenon of female ejaculation has led to a relaxing of this taboo. Although you'll still occasionally see a big, black censorship box pasted over images of female ejaculation, you can now rent adult videos such as the "Oh My Gush!" and "Rainwoman" series, which string together scene after scene of squirting.

Certainly when ejaculation is a gimmick in a porn film, there's no guaranteeing authenticity. In some videos, it practically looks as though the producers have hooked a garden hose up between the actress' legs. However, there are a few stars who are justly lauded for their hot, wet performances. Look for Sarah-Jane Hamilton in mainstream videos and Carol Queen in alternative and educational films.

Is it safe?

Female ejaculate is a bodily fluid, so you may well be wondering whether or not it's risky for ejaculate to come into contact with mucous membranes. However, a call to the Centers for Disease Control will get you no definitive answers as to ejaculate's relative risks as a transmission fluid for HIV, because (are you surprised?) there have been no studies as to the amount of HIV present in female ejaculate.

Vaginal fluids contain a relatively low concentration of HIV, but they are still considered a transmission fluid. Urine is not considered a transmission fluid, as it contains HIV only in trace amounts. This leaves the jury out with regard to female ejaculate. While there's certainly no danger in ejaculating on unbroken skin, it's up to the individual to decide whether he or she wishes to avoid unprotected oral and genital contact with female fluids.

Is it healthy?

There's some evidence for the theory that ejaculating may reduce your chances of getting cystitis, or at least relieve the symptoms of bladder infections.[50] A 1996 article in the *Journal of Western Medicine* suggests that female urethral syndrome (a "wastebasket" term for conditions such as cystitis) is comparable to male prostatitis.[51] In both cases, bacterial infections can clog up the prostatic ducts, inflaming the glands, and resulting in frequent, painful urination.

As any man who's had a prostate infection can testify, doctor's orders include a course of regular ejaculation—ejaculation helps flush out the prostatic ducts. Presumably ejaculating women can help ward off bladder infections by "flushing" their urethral glands and ducts on a regular basis. Preventative health care can be fun.

How can I be sure I'm ejaculating?

While awareness of female ejaculation is infiltrating the mainstream through articles in women's magazines and brief references in sex manuals, many women are still unsure whether they are actually ejaculating or urinating. Sometimes this is due to ignorance.

There was a big wet spot on the bed (as big as a saucer or a salad plate) that my lover said came from me. I smelled it cautiously when he left for a washcloth, and it definitely was not urine. I had never heard about female ejaculation and I figured there was something wrong with me—that I was strange and weird and somehow flawed.

Sometimes it's due to a gap between what we believe is possible in the abstract and what we believe we're capable of as sexual individuals. It can be difficult to match our subjective perceptions with the expectations generated by what we read or hear about sex.

I've questioned whether or not I really had an ejaculation. I know that it didn't feel like urination, however the sensations are so mingled in that area during sex, it seems to be easy to miss exactly what is going on.

We tend to expect that our sexual experiences will adhere to some common formula, some definable "norm." Yet, if the history of attitudes about female ejaculation teaches us nothing else, it teaches us that the "norm" is continually being redefined. Whether the fluids you produce during sex are vaginal fluids, female ejaculate or urine is less important than allowing yourself to experience a full range of sensations without suppressing your responses. After all, sex isn't just good clean fun, it's good slippery fun.

I love to get very wet, and my partner likes it as well.

Ebb and Flow

As with many sexual responses, it seems that female ejaculation and sensitivity to G-spot stimulation can vary depending on hormonal influences. The urethral sponge has been reported to be smaller in post-menopausal women,[52] and studies have shown enzymatic differences between the urethral sponge in pre- and post-menopausal women.[53]

However, there's been very little formal research on the influence of hormones on the urethral sponge and ejaculation. Anecdotally, women do report that G-spot sensitivity—as well as the amount, texture, smell and taste of their ejaculate—fluctuates along with the hormonal fluctuations of the menstrual cycle and during pregnancy.

It varies according to where I am in my cycle. Usually about a week before my menstrual flow begins is when I tend to experience ejaculation more.

I've found that G-spot sensitivity increases a great deal during pregnancy and ovulation.

Right before menstruating, my G-spot is extremely sensitive.

Certainly a variety of physiological and emotional changes can contribute to changes in sexual response, often in unexpected ways.

The ejaculations—wow!—have been very frequent over the last several months. It might be because I'm taking Prozac, which seems to have reduced the sensitivity of all my erectile tissues (my nipples and clitoris don't feel as much as usual and don't get that hard). Now, rather than coming quickly from the clitoris, perhaps I'm staying aroused long enough to experience ejaculation. I also have a tireless partner—no small blessing.

Some women find that a hysterectomy affects all kinds of sexual responses and may reduce G-spot sensitivity. It's important that any woman contemplating a hysterectomy inform her doctor about her particular vaginal sensitivities, so that the doctor can use this information in making surgical decisions.

The first ob/gyn I consulted about my hysterectomy insisted on removing my cervix—she saw the cervix as "cancer producing" and thought I was silly to want to leave it in. I was fortunate enough to get a second consultation with a wonderful ob/gyn who asked, "Do you have vaginal orgasms?" When I said yes, she immediately suggested I have a supra-cervical hysterectomy (leaving the cervix in). She said she'd learned her lesson from a previous patient who told her that a hysterectomy had destroyed her sex life. We need more doctors like this.

Other women find that a hysterectomy either doesn't affect their sexual responses, or produces positive changes. If organs are removed, but the nerves and muscles are left intact, sexual responsiveness need not be affected.

I had surgically-induced menopause at a young age (via hysterectomy). My level of desire and responsiveness has greatly increased since my hysterectomy. And I still have a G-spot. Some women are afraid they won't feel the same sexually after surgery—but I feel better.

I've only been having G-spot orgasms since I became menopausal. I do know that the hysterectomy I had a year ago has changed my responsiveness. Now that I don't feel my womb's contractions with arousal and during orgasm, I am much more attuned to my G-spot.

Tips, Toys and Techniques

Now that you've got the lay of the land, it's time to discuss some of the ways in which you and your partner can enhance your enjoyment of G-spot stimulation and female ejaculation.

About the PC Muscle

The pubococcygeus muscles have an important role to play in sexual pleasure. This group of muscles lies an inch or two beneath the pelvic floor in both men and women, and runs from the pubic bone to the tailbone, encircling the vagina (or base of the penis), urethra and rectum. The pubococcygeus muscle group is generally referred to as the PC muscle for short. The PC naturally contracts during orgasm, and learning to voluntarily control this muscle can greatly enhance sexual arousal and response.

A well-toned muscle is a more responsive muscle, and in the case of the PC muscle, good tone can result in increased sexual sensation. When you contract the PC muscle, you temporarily reduce the flow of blood in the surrounding area. Once you release the muscle, the flow of blood into the genital tissue increases, producing greater vaginal lubrication in women, stronger erections in men and a heightened genital awareness that can be quite arousing.

The erogenous potential of the pelvic muscles is well known in many cultures. The isolation of individual muscles of the pelvis and abdomen is integral to belly dancing, hula and certain styles of African dance. Yet in the Western world, we owe our awareness of the power of the PC to one trailblazing gynecologist of the 1940s, Arnold Kegel.

Dr. Kegel developed a series of simple exercises for the PC muscle to assist women with urinary stress incontinence. He reasoned that strengthening the muscles of the pelvic floor would allow his patients greater bladder control, sparing them the surgical, drug or electrode treatments that were the order of the day. Kegel's patients soon found that strengthening the PC muscle not only reduced their incontinence, it also improved their sex lives. Many of these women had their first orgasms as a result of their training, while others reported that improved muscle tone led to stronger orgasms and greater vaginal sensitivity.

PC muscle exercises are now generically referred to as "Kegels" in Dr. Kegel's honor. They are used in treating incontinence and in preparing for childbirth. And they offer a deliciously simple route to enhanced sexual sensation. Improved PC muscle tone results in stronger erections, greater control over the timing of ejaculation, greater genital sensitivity, increased lubrication in women, increased orgasmic response and peace on earth (okay, peace on earth is purely speculative).

To do Kegel exercises, you first need to learn to isolate the PC muscle. The classic way to do so is to practice stopping and starting the flow of urine—the muscle you contract and release in this process is the PC muscle.

Start with a series of flicks, briefly contracting and releasing the muscle. If you're a woman, think of bringing the walls of your vagina together in a kiss. If you're a man, think of doing "penis-lifts." Over time, you can build up to doing as many as 100 contractions at a stretch.

Once you've mastered these brief rhythmic contractions, practice holding the contraction for longer and longer time periods. Or slowly contract your PC muscle as you inhale, and then slowly bear down with the muscle as you exhale.

You can do these Kegels anytime and any place in order to increase flexibility. However, if you'd like to build the muscle, your best bet would be to exercise with some sort of resistive device in your vagina or rectum—a finger or a dildo will work equally well. Try reaching about one to two inches into your vagina or rectum, and you should be able to feel the band of the PC muscle beneath the surface.

Bear in mind that it's just as important to learn how to consciously relax the muscle as to flex it. Having a chronically tense, tight PC muscle is not necessarily better than having a weak muscle. Your goal is voluntary control, not a vise-like grip.

Experiment with contracting and releasing your PC muscle during sex. As your vagina becomes more lubricated, and your erectile tissues expand, you'll probably feel heightened vaginal sensitivity and greater awareness of the G-spot area. As we noted in the last chapter, female ejaculators tend to have strong PC muscles. If you feel on the verge of ejaculating, bear down with your PC muscle, and you may be able to voluntarily eject your ejaculate.

I recently started experiencing a gush of clear fluid with orgasm (usually from internal stimulation, but not always). The orgasm usually has to involve voluntary contraction of the PC muscle.

About "G-spot Orgasms"

Much of the hype around the G-spot revolves around the notion that it's the magic key that opens the gates to honest-to-goodness vaginal orgasms. As we've noted previously, it's somewhat arbitrary to employ terms such as "clitoral orgasm" and "vaginal orgasm" given the intimate interconnection between all the structures of the female genitals. Furthermore, these labels have caused considerable anxiety to generations of women, who worry that they're having the "wrong kind" of orgasm.

We've never met an orgasm we didn't like, and we're reluctant to apply labels. When it comes to sex, it's often a short step from making distinctions to organizing sexual experience into a hierarchy of good, better and best. Ours is a competitive society, and at Good Vibrations we spend a lot of time urging people to respect their own responses, rather than following some magazine article's "seven steps to bigger, better orgasms."

However, while we refuse to identify any one orgasm as "better" than another, we also recognize that no two orgasms are alike. Women who enjoy G-spot stimulation and/or who ejaculate do report that the resulting orgasms feel qualitatively different from those triggered primarily by clitoral stimulation.

To ejaculate, I need prolonged sexual arousal followed by longer stimulation. When I do ejaculate, it feels awesome, more "total body" than a regular orgasm.

Two of the authors of *The G Spot,* John Perry and Beverly Whipple, have presented an interesting theory to account for the varieties of orgasmic experience. They speculate that two different nerve pathways participate in sexual response, and that subjective perceptions of different types of orgasm are based on whether one or both of these pathways are involved in the orgasm.

The two nerve pathways are the pudendal nerve and the pelvic nerve, both of which play a role in male sexual response.[54] Kinsey and Masters and Johnson all felt, however, that female orgasm was exclusively triggered by the clitoral glans, which is connected to the pudendal nerve. Ladas, Perry and Whipple suggest that the pelvic nerve comes into play during G-spot stimulation and ejaculation, and the fact that signals travel to the brain along an additional nerve pathway accounts for the different sensations described by women who experience orgasm this way.[55]

In the model of female orgasm documented by Masters and Johnson, the clitoral glans is the focal point for stimulation and the pudendal nerve is the pathway. As excitement builds, the PC muscle contracts, the lower third of the vagina congests with blood, and the uterus lifts up, resulting in a ballooning effect in the upper two-thirds of the vagina. Upon orgasm, tension is discharged through the PC muscle, producing rhythmic contractions in the outer third of the vagina and surrounding tissues.

In the alternate model of female orgasm proposed by Ladas, Perry and Whipple, the G-spot is the focal point for stimulation and the pelvic nerve (which connects to the G-spot, bladder and uterus) serves as the pathway. Upon orgasm, tension is discharged through muscles of the uterus, bladder and the deeper portion of the PC muscle, which is closer to the uterus. This involvement of "inner" rather than "outer" muscles could explain why many women describe G-spot and ejaculatory orgasms as feeling particularly "deep."[56]

Orgasm with ejaculation is somehow a deeper release than a non-ejaculatory orgasm, and is usually more intense. The best analogy I can offer is great music on a powerful stereo: a non-ejaculating orgasm is like the mid-range frequencies, and an orgasm with ejaculation is like adding in both the top of the treble and lots of bass!!

The Male G-spot

The G-spot is often referred to as the female prostate, and conversely the prostate could well be thought of as the male G-spot. After all, they both evolve from the same embryonic tissue, and both are potential erogenous zones. As with the G-spot, you're more likely to enjoy prostate stimulation after you're already sexually aroused, and pressure on the prostate initially triggers the urge to urinate, followed by pleasurable sensations.

In both sexes, the prostate can be stimulated either externally (by pressing against the perineum in men or against the urethral opening in women) or internally. You can locate the male prostate internally by pressing through the front wall of the rectum about three inches in, just as you locate the G-spot by pressing through the front wall of the vagina. In both cases, it can be difficult to hit the spot yourself, and a friend's fingers, dildo or penis are handy helpers.

Many men can orgasm solely from prostate stimulation. Some men distinguish between orgasms triggered by penile stimulation and those triggered by prostate stimulation. Like G-spot orgasms, prostate-triggered orgasms are often described as "deep" and "full-bodied." The difference in sensation is enhanced by the fact that the prostate connects to the pelvic nerve pathway and the penis to the pudendal and pelvic nerve pathways.

Actually, just as vaginal and G-spot stimulation result in indirect stimulation of the clitoral legs, prostate stimulation results in indirect stimulation of the root of the penis. Just as women may enjoy "blended" orgasms from stimulating the clitoris and G-spot, men can enjoy powerful blends of sexual sensation from stimulating the penis and prostate simultaneously. And many of the toys that are designed for G-spot massage do excellent double-duty as prostate toys.

As excitement builds, women experiencing orgasms from G-spot stimulation frequently experience a bearing-down sensation: the uterus moves down, the upper vagina tightens, and the PC muscle relaxes, expanding the vaginal opening.[57] If you're a woman who ejaculates, this bearing-down motion is probably familiar to you, and if you or your partner have ever watched what's going on, you may have noted the acorn-like protrusion around the urethra visibly pushing out.

You've probably noticed that the PC muscle has a part to play in both types of orgasm. The PC is primarily connected to the pudendal nerve, but the deeper part of the PC is connected to the pelvic nerve, as are the muscles of the uterus. The authors of *The G Spot* speculate that individual variances in how these two nerve pathways serve the PC muscle may help explain individual variances in orgasmic response.[58]

These theories of orgasm may or may not correspond with your personal experience. As in all things related to sex, the reality of women's experience doesn't always fall into tidy categories, and we wouldn't want it to. You may experience one type of orgasm that suits you just fine; you may make very clear distinctions between what you think of as "clitoral" or "vaginal" orgasms; or you may routinely enjoy a combination of sensations—what some sexologists refer to as "blended" orgasms.[59] After all, while the glans of the clitoris is connected to the pudendal nerve, the clitoral shaft and legs are connected to the pelvic nerve.[60] It's highly likely that different types of clitoral stimulation can produce different sensations of orgasm. And it's highly *unlikely* that you'd ever be stimulating one portion of your genitals exclusively.

The bottom line is, if you're willing to experiment with new types of stimulation, you'll probably discover a wide range of new sensations to enjoy.

This is going to get poetic, but female ejaculation feels like several waves of sheer delight that come one right after another, followed by a euphoric feeling. I have been left so relaxed in the aftermath of one of these experiences that I was completely unwilling to move for about fifteen minutes.

When I stimulate my G-spot, I feel a voracious, frantic excitement: "More! More!" When I stimulate the spot near my cervix, it's a sweet feeling, and I'm happy to experience each moment slowly: "Yes, Yes." Both types of stimu-

lation can trigger orgasm, but when the G-spot triggers orgasm, it's much more intense.

Toys

One person's sexual discovery is another person's commercial opportunity, and the publication of *The G Spot* launched a slew of products all ostensibly designed to help the women of America hit the spot. Before the early '80s, nearly all insertable toys were ramrod straight. The best thing about the trend in G-spot products is that manufacturers are now producing insertable vibrators and dildos that are curved to match the natural shape of the vagina and rectum.

When playing with any insertable vaginal toy, it's a good idea to smooth the way with a water-based lubricant. When playing with any insertable anal toy, lubricant is essential, as the delicate tissue of the rectum doesn't produce any natural lubrication of its own. And if you're playing with an anal toy, make sure it's either long enough that you won't let go of the handle or, preferably, that it has a flared base and can't slip inside the rectum.

Vibrators

You may or may not find a vibrator a useful G-spot toy. Some women feel that vibrations distract from G-spot stimulation, while others find they are the perfect way to amplify arousal. The G-spot is responsive to pressure, not touch, so there's no guarantee that you'll find internal vibration particularly stimulating. On the other hand, vibrators certainly do the trick when it comes to external G-spot stimulation. For instance, if you press a vibrator against the clitoris and mouth of the urethra, the sensations can be transmitted to the urethral sponge inside, causing your G-spot to swell.

I always ejaculate the same way—by using my Prelude vibrator on the shaft of my clitoris and nothing else.

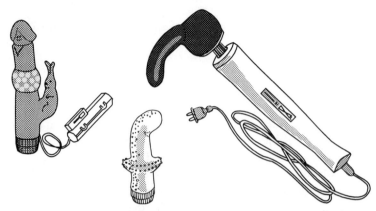

I press one Smoothie battery vibrator against the front wall of my vagina from the inside and another against my vaginal lips. It's easiest to reach orgasm when the outer toy is almost mirroring the location of the inner toy.

G-spot attachments are available for electric massagers—these fit over the head of wand vibrators and onto the shaft of coil-operated vibrators. In the case of the G-spotter attachment that fits over the head of the Hitachi Magic Wand, there's a delightful dual vibration effect. The insertable portion of the attachment stimulates the vagina or rectum, while the vibrating head of the wand can be pressed against the clitoris or perineum.

There are a multitude of battery-operated G-spot vibrators on the market. These tend to be generic phallic-shaped vibrators, with a curve at the tip. Again, we can't promise that these will provide strong enough vibrations to effectively stimulate your G-spot. However, battery vibrators are available in such a wide range of lengths, widths and materials, you may well find one that's a handy and inexpensive tool for locating the G-spot.

I wish I had a vibrator that had the right curve and was hard enough and circled like a finger! I have one that is supposedly a G-spot vibrator, but it isn't that effective (I need a lot of pressure).

The customer quoted above might want to check one of the dual-operated premium battery vibrators such as the Beaver or Rabbit Pearl.

These feature a rotating insertable shaft on which is mounted a vibrating clitoral attachment. In certain models such as the Rabbit Pearl, tumbling plastic pearls in the midsection of the shaft provide potential stimulation to the G-spot.

Dildos

Dildos are probably the most popular G-spot toy around (second only to fingers), as many women find it easiest to focus attention on the sensitive areas of the vagina when there's something inside them.

I like flexible, slim dildos. It's best if I move, squeezing the dildo, while it stays still.

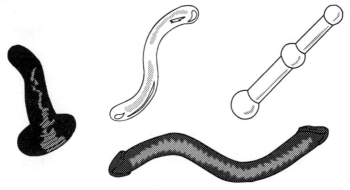

There are so many styles of curved dildos on the market that you're bound to find one with the angle that suits you best. In fact, one of the latest developments in dildo technology is a flexible plastic spine inserted into rubber dildos, which allows you to bend the dildo to your own specifications. Double dildos also offer the advantages of length and maneuverability, which, as the customer quoted below suggests, are desirable traits in a G-spot toy.

I'd like to see more toys that could be manipulated by one person lying on the back—perhaps having long, curved handles.

Since you need to press through the wall of the vagina to contact the G-spot, it's a good idea to select a dildo that's fairly firm. Two of the most popular G-spot toys around are made of extremely hard materials.

The first of these is the Kegelcisor, a "vaginal barbell" made of surgical steel, set with three spheres of varying diameters. The Kegelcisor was designed as a resistive device for practicing Kegel exercises (the idea being that as you build muscle tone, you practice squeezing your PC muscle around increasingly smaller spheres). A lot of women find that the Kegelcisor's knob fits nicely behind the pubic bone, that its slim size makes it easy to angle against the front wall of the vagina, and that its weight and heft provide ideal pressure against the G-spot.

The Crystal Wand is designed explicitly as a G-spot and prostate toy. It's a slim, elegant lucite dildo molded into an S-shape. You can easily hold one end with your hand and maneuver the other end to press against the front wall of the vagina or rectum.

I hook the Crystal Wand over my pubic bone and jiggle it against my G-spot while pressing my Magic Wand vibrator on my clit and labia. The first time I tried these two toys together, the pleasure was so intense I nearly fell off the bed!

Women who ejaculate frequently use dildos to stimulate the urethral sponge. But don't be surprised if, when you ejaculate, the bearing-down motion of the PC muscle ejects any toy (or body part) you might have had inside.

Improvise

Please don't feel restricted to toys with "G-spot" on the label. You're in the best position to figure out what props give you pleasure. Some women find that tucking a small object, such as Ben-Wa balls, against the G-spot is the optimal way to get stimulation.

Ejaculation is ridiculously easy for me lately. When I'm alone, the best way is to combine Ben-Wa balls with a vibrator against my clitoris and labia while lying on my back.

*I use Duotone Balls and move them in and out near the
entrance of my vagina, pressing against the G-spot.*

Others are inspired to design their own toys.

*I still haven't found a way to hit the G-spot reliably myself.
I once had a dream about a device like a curved pencil
with a rubber tip that I think would work, but I
haven't ever seen anything like it.*

Experiment

If you're not someone who enjoys G-spot stimulation or who ejaculates,
we're not going to pretend that a G-spot toy will change your tune. And
even if you are, these toys may not make their way into your standard
repertoire. Either way, you've got nothing to lose by experimenting with
vibrators and dildos, and it's entirely possible they'll turn you on to a
whole new world of pleasure.

End Note

We hope you've found the information in this book both useful and thought-provoking, and that it answered your questions about the G-spot and female ejaculation. If what you've read inspires you to experiment with new types of stimulation for yourself or a partner, more power to you. All we ask is that you approach your sexual explorations with a playful spirit.

Accurate sex information is hard to come by, and we applaud you for seeking it out. We're all forced to wade through an confusing blend of fact and fiction regarding the simple facts of human sexuality—at the same time, we receive next to no training in communicating about our sexual desires and preferences.

At Good Vibrations, we've been in the business of offering straight talk about sex for over twenty years. We've had the pleasure of learning as much from our customers and friends as they learn from us, and the one lesson that's brought home to us over and over again is that honest communication about sex leads to greater health and happiness.

We encourage you to spread a sex-positive message in whatever way feels appropriate to you. Share the information in this book with a friend or loved one. Speak up to correct misperceptions when you hear them. If the history of attitudes about the G-spot and female ejaculation has one thing to teach us, it's that blanket theories of sexuality never tell the whole story. The wide variety in individual sexual response and experience is a richer and infinitely more fascinating tale.

Notes

1. Mark A. Winton, "Editorial: The Social Construction of the G-Spot and Female Ejaculation," *Journal of Sex Education & Therapy*, 15 (1989), p. 151.

2. Alfred C. Kinsey et al., *Sexual Behavior in the Human Female* (Philadelphia: W.B. Saunders Company, 1953), p. 584.

3. Robert T. Michael et al., *Sex in America: A Definitive Survey* (Boston: Little, Brown and Company, 1994), p. 128.

4. June M. Reinisch with Ruth Beasley, *The Kinsey Institute New Report on Sex* (New York: St. Martin's Press, 1990), p. 201.

5. Ibid., p. 203.

6. Whipple, Beverly, William E. Hartman and Marilyn A. Fithian, "Orgasm" in *Human Sexuality: An Encyclopedia*, ed. Vern L. Bullough and Bonnie Bullough (New York: Garland Publishing, 1994), p. 432.

7. *See* Milan Zaviacic and Beverly Whipple, "Update on the Female Prostate and the Phenomenon of Female Ejaculation," *The Journal of Sex Research*, 30 (May 1993), pp. 148-151, for a summary.

8. Ibid., p. 150.

9. Federation of Feminist Women's Health Centers, *A New View of a Woman's Body* (New York: Simon and Schuster, 1981), p. 47.

10. Kinsey, pp. 574-584.

11. Ibid., p. 580.

12. Ibid., p. 592.

13. Ernst Grafenberg and Robert L. Dickinson, "Conception Control by Plastic Cervix Cap," quoted in Alice Kahn Ladas, Beverly Whipple, and John D. Perry, *The G Spot: And Other Recent Discoveries About Human Sexuality* (New York: Dell Publishers, 1982), p. 53.

14. Ernst Grafenberg, "The Role of the Urethra in Female Orgasm," *International Journal of Sexology*, 3 (1950), p. 146.

15. Carol Tavris, *Mismeasure of Woman* (New York: Simon & Schuster, 1992), p. 236.

16. John D. Perry and Beverly Whipple, "Pelvic Muscle Strength of Female Ejaculators: Evidence in Support of a New Theory of Orgasm," cited by Beverly Whipple and Barry R. Komisaruk, "The G Spot, Orgasm and Female Ejaculation: Are They Related?" in *The Proceedings of the First International Conference on Orgasm*, ed. P. Kothari (Bombay: VRP Publishers, 1991), p. 229.

17. Ladas, Whipple and Perry, p. 43.

18. Ibid., p. 42.

19. Ibid., pp. 20-21.

20. Cited by Whipple and Komisaruk, p. 229.

21. Whipple and Komisaruk, pp. 229-230.

22. Ladas, Alice Kahn,"The G Spot," *American Academy of Clinical Sexologists Clinical Monograph*, 3 (1997), p. 1.

23. *See* Zaviacic and Whipple for a summary.

24. Galen, *On the Usefulness of the Parts*, quoted in Josephine Lowndes Sevely, *Eve's Secrets: A New Theory of Female Sexuality* (New York: Random House, 1987, out of print), pp. 50-51.

25. *Kama Sutra of Vatsyayana*, translated by Sir Richard F. Burton (New York: E.P. Dutton, 1962), p. 91.

26. Sevely, p. 66.

27. *The Perfumed Garden*, translated by Sir Richard Burton (Rochester: Park Street Press, 1992), p. 30.

28. Sevely, pp. 67-68; Ladas, Whipple and Perry, pp. 74-79.

29. J.J. Stewart, "The Myth of Female Ejaculation, Female Prostate and the Grafenberg Spot," cited by Bonnie Bullough et al. in "Subjective Reports of Female Orgasmic Expulsion of Fluid," *Nurse Practitioner* (March 1984), p. 56, n. 15.

30. Regnier De Graaf, *New Treatise Concerning the Generative Organs of Women*, quoted in Sevely, pp. 71-74.

31. Thomas Laqueur, author of *Making Sex: Body and Gender from the Greeks to Freud*, quoted in Canadian Broadcasting Corp. radio program, "Ideas: One Sex or Two?" (Toronto: CBC Radio Works, 1995).

32. Ladas, Whipple and Perry, p. 78.

33. Grafenberg, p. 147.

34. Kinsey, pp. 634-635.

35. Quoted in Canadian Broadcasting Corp. radio program, "Ideas: One Sex or Two?"

36. Ladas, Whipple and Perry, pp. 37-38; Grafenberg, p. 148.

37. *The Perfumed Garden*, p. 38.

38. Ladas, Whipple and Perry, p. 53; Grafenberg, p. 147.

39. Perry and Whipple, cited by Whipple and Komisaruk, p. 229.

40. Milan Zaviacic, et al., "Female Urethral Expulsions Evoked by Local Digital Stimulation of the G-spot: Differences in the Response Patterns," cited by Whipple and Komisaruk, pp. 229-232.

41. John D. Perry and Beverly Whipple, "Pelvic Muscle Strength of Female Ejaculators: Evidence in Support of a New Theory of Orgasm," cited by Ladas, Whipple and Perry, p. 122.

42. Beverly Whipple, quoted in Canadian Broadcasting Corp. radio program, "Ideas: One Sex or Two?"

43. Ladas, Whipple and Perry, p. 60.

44. Bonnie Bullough et al., p. 58.

45. J. K. Davidson, C. A. Darling and C. Conway-Welch, "The Role of the Grafenberg Spot and Female Ejaculation in the Female Orgasmic Response: An Empirical Analysis;" and Beverly Whipple's unpublished Female Sexual Health Questionnaire, cited by Whipple and Komisaruk, p. 233.

46. *See* Zaviacic and Whipple for a summary.

47. Gary Schubach, "Urethral Expulsions during Sensual Arousal and Bladder Catheterization in Seven Human Females" (Doctoral research project, EdD, The Institute for Advanced Study of Human Sexuality, 1996), p. 39.

48. Ibid., p. 40.

49. Ladas, Whipple and Perry, p. 69; Sevely, p. 92; Schubach, p. 38.

50. Ladas, Whipple and Perry, pp. 80-81.

51. Dr. Ruben Gittes and Dr. Robert M. Nakemure, paper in *Journal of Western Medicine* (May 1996), cited by a posting to the Society for Human Sexuality web site.

52. Ladas, Whipple and Perry, p. 82.

53. Zaviacic and Whipple, p. 149.

54. Bullough et al., p. 55.

55. *See* Ladas, Whipple and Perry, pp. 147-153 for a summary of Perry and Whipple's studies. The hypogastric plexus is also involved in transmitting sensation from the G-spot and uterus.

56. Ibid.

57. Ibid., p. 145. Perry and Whipple refer to this as the "A-Frame-effect."

58. Ibid., p. 90. The hypogastric plexus also serves the deeper part of the PC muscle.

59. Josephine and Irving Singer, "Types of Female Orgasm," cited by Ladas, Whipple and Perry, pp. 148-153. The Singers theorize that there are three types of female orgasm: "vulval," (or clitoral); "uterine," (or vaginal); and "blended," (a combination). Perry and Whipple expand this theory to propose a continuum of female orgasm, in which most women experience some type of "blended" orgasm.

60. Ladas, Whipple and Perry, p. 136.

References

Books

Federation of Feminist Women's Health Centers. *A New View of a Woman's Body*. New York: Simon and Schuster, 1981.

Kama Sutra of Vatsyayana. Translated by Sir Richard F. Burton. New York: E.P. Dutton, 1962.

Kinsey, Alfred C.; Pomeroy, Wardell B.; Martin, Clyde E.; and Gebhard, Paul H. *Sexual Behavior in the Human Female*. Philadelphia: W.B. Saunders Company, 1953.

Ladas, Alice Kahn; Whipple, Beverly; and Perry, John D. *The G Spot: And Other Recent Discoveries About Human Sexuality*. New York: Dell Publishers, 1982.

Michael, Robert T.; Gagnon, John H.; Laumann, Edward O.; and Kolata, Gina. *Sex in America: A Definitive Survey*. Boston: Little, Brown and Company, 1994.

The Pearl. New York: Grove Press, 1968.

The Perfumed Garden. Translated by Sir Richard F. Burton. Rochester: Park Street Press, 1992.

Reinisch, June M with Beasley, Ruth. *The Kinsey Institute New Report on Sex*. New York: St. Martin's Press, 1990.

Sevely, Josephine Lowndes. *Eve's Secrets: A New Theory of Female Sexuality*. New York: Random House, 1987, o/p.

Tavris, Carol. *Mismeasure of Woman*. New York: Simon & Schuster, 1992.

Other References

Canadian Broadcasting Corp. radio program, "Ideas: One Sex or Two?" Toronto: CBC Radio Works, 15 February 1995.

Bullough, Bonnie; Davis, Madeline; Whipple, Beverly; Dixon, Joan; Allgeier, Elizabeth; and Drury, Kate. "Subjective Reports of Female Orgasmic Expulsion of Fluid." *Nurse Practitioner* (March 1984): 55-58.

Grafenberg, Ernst. "The Role of the Urethra in Female Orgasm." *International Journal of Sexology*, 3 (1950): 145-148.

Ladas, Alice Kahn. "The G Spot." *The American Academy of Clinical Sexologists Clinical Monograph*, 3 (1997): 1-4.

Schubach, Gary. "Urethral Expulsions during Sensual Arousal and Bladder Catheterization in Seven Human Females." Doctoral Research Project, EdD, The Institute for Advanced Study of Human Sexuality, San Francisco, 1996.

Whipple, Beverly. "G Spot and Female Pleasure." in *Human Sexuality: An Encyclopedia*, pp. 229-232. Edited by Vern L. Bullough and Bonnie Bullough. New York: Garland Publishing, 1994.

Whipple, Beverly; Hartman, William E.; and Fithian, Marilyn A. "Orgasm" in *Human Sexuality: An Encyclopedia*, pp. 430-433. Edited by Vern L. Bullough and Bonnie Bullough. New York: Garland Publishing, 1994.

Whipple, Beverly and Komisaruk, Barry R. "The G Spot, Orgasm and Female Ejaculation: Are They Related?" in *The Proceedings of the First International Conference on Orgasm*, pp. 227-237. Edited by P. Kothari. Bombay: VRP Publishers, 1991.

Winton, Mark A. "Editorial: The Social Construction of the G-Spot and Female Ejaculation." *Journal of Sex Education & Therapy*, 15 (1989): 151-162.

Zaviacic, Milan and Whipple, Beverly. "Update on the Female Prostate and the Phenomenon of Female Ejaculation." *The Journal of Sex Research*, 30 (May 1993): 148-151.

Resources

Bibliography

Federation of Feminist Women's Health Centers. *A New View of a Woman's Body.* New York: Simon and Schuster, 1981. A classic of the women's self-help movement, featuring color photos and Suzann Gage's illustrations of female genitals.

Ladas, Alice Kahn, Whipple, Beverly and Perry, John D. *The G Spot: And Other Recent Discoveries About Human Sexuality.* New York: Dell Publishers, 1982. Still the most comprehensive and readable book about the G-spot, female ejaculation and varieties of orgasm.

Sevely, Josephine Lowndes. *Eve's Secrets: A New Theory of Female Sexuality.* New York: Random House, 1987, out of print. Offers an enthralling historical review of literature about the female prostate and female ejaculation as well as a provocative argument for the fundamental symmetry between female and male genitals. Look for this at used bookstores or at the library.

Winks, Cathy and Semans, Anne. *The New Good Vibrations Guide to Sex.* San Francisco: Cleis Press, (1994) 1997. The most complete sex manual ever written offers explicit, expert advice on oral sex, intercourse, masturbation, fantasy exploration and tips for playing with every variety of sex toy.

Videography

Educational Videos

Carol Queen's Great Vibrations, directed by Joani Blank (Blank Tapes, 1995). Carol Queen, a Good Vibrations staffer and sex educator, offers a comprehensive introduction to the wonderful world of vibrators. Her explicit demonstrations include tips on G-spot stimulation and scenes of female ejaculation.

How to Female Ejaculate (Fatale, 1992). Fanny Fatale reviews female anatomy before she, Carol Queen, Shannon Bell and Baja sit down for some girl talk about the G-spot and ejaculation. All four women demonstrate their ejaculation techniques and show off their favorite G-spot toys in a compelling group masturbation scene. The only flaws in this landmark video are erratic sound quality and the emphasis that "any woman can" ejaculate if she just tries hard enough.

The Incredible G-spot, directed by Laura Corn (Merlin/Park Avenue Publishers, 1995). Popular sex writer Laura Corn hosts a G-spot infomercial with four heterosexual couples, sharing her tips and techniques for combining clitoral and vaginal stimulation. Computer graphics are put to good use in diagrams of female genitals.

Includes demonstrations of intercourse positions that offer G-spot stimulation, but no demonstrations of ejaculation.

Nice Girls Don't Do It, directed by Kathy Daymond (1990). An experimental art film that isn't commercially available, *Nice Girls* is an audio-visual montage in which Shannon Bell explicates and demonstrates her ejaculation techniques.

Sluts and Goddesses, directed by Maria Beatty and Annie Sprinkle (1992). Annie's video workshop includes one scene of "moonflower drops of wisdom," aka female ejaculation.

Videos for Lovers: Behind the Bedroom Door: Donna and Gary (Educational Video Corp., 1996). In this volume of a popular series in which ordinary lovers talk in explicit detail about their sex lives and then demonstrate the activities they discuss, Donna and Gary share their experience with female ejaculation (as well as anal stimulation, cock rings and vibrators).

Adult Videos
Hundreds of new adult videos are released every week. The following are a handful of noteworthy titles that include either G-spot information or authentic scenes of female ejaculation.

Clips (Fatale Video, 1988). The three short vignettes in this lesbian-made video depict anal masturbation, safe-sex bondage and an awesome female ejaculation scene starring Fanny Fatale.

The Grafenberg Spot (Mitchell Brothers, 1985) is a tongue-in-cheek romp, starring Ginger Lynn. When she ejaculates on lover Harry Reems during oral sex, he thinks she's peeing on him. Can this relationship be saved? Thanks to the explicit advice of sex therapist Annette Haven, it can. John Holmes also stars. The copious ejaculations are faked (watch the entertaining outtakes for details), but the humorous approach to communication issues is a genuine delight.

I Touch Myself (Immaculate Video Conceptions, 1994). Six porn actresses, including Tyffany Million, Sarah-Jane Hamilton and Isis Nile, detail their masturbation fantasies and enthusiastically demonstrate their favorite techniques. Sarah-Jane Hamilton ejaculates.

Masturbation Memoirs (House O'Chicks, 1995). This independently-produced video celebrates authentic sexual experience. Six different women speak about their sexual histories and demonstrate their favorite masturbation techniques. Sexual revolutionary Annie Sprinkle explains "medabation," her approach to masturbatory enlightenment, and ejaculates.

Mind Games (Immaculate Video Conceptions, 1995). Tyffany Million portrays a frustrated writer drawn into the sexual fantasies she overhears from a neighboring office. Sarah-Jane Hamilton shines as the college roomie who explodes into orgasm and ejaculation after an innocent wrestling match with Million turns into a sizzling penetration scene. Directed by Wesley Emerson.

Pretending (Cal Vista, 1994). A bored husband spices up his monogamous marriage by imagining his lovely wife getting down and dirty with guests at a tedious business dinner. His vivid fantasies include several authentic orgasms and ejaculations from Sarah-Jane Hamilton. Directed by Paul Thomas.

Real Women, Real Fantasies (1993). Veronica Monet's independently-produced video sets out to capture the erotic experiences of five real women, who share their fantasies and demonstrate how they achieve mindblowing orgasms. Veronica ejaculates.

Toys and Information

Stores and mail order:

Adam & Eve, catalog
PO Box 800
Carrboro, NC 27510
919/644-1212
800/274-0333
http://www.adameve.com

Blowfish, catalog
2261 Market Street, #284
San Francisco, CA 94114
800/325-2569
http://www.blowfish.com

Eve's Garden, store and catalog
119 West 57th Street, #420
New York, NY 10019-2383
212/757-8651
800/848-3837
http://www.evesgarden.com

The Good Vibrations catalog features sex toys and a sampling of videos.

Good Vibrations, catalogs
938 Howard Street, #101
San Francisco, CA 94103
415/974-8990
800/289-8423
http://www.goodvibes.com

Good Vibrations, store
603 Valencia Street
San Francisco, CA 94110
415/522-5460

Good Vibrations, store
1620 Polk Street
San Francisco, CA 94109
415/345-0400

Good Vibrations, store
2504 San Pablo Avenue
Berkeley, CA 94702
510/841-8987

Grand Opening!, store and catalog
318 Harvard Street, Suite 32
Arcade Building, Coolidge Corner
Brookline, MA 02146
617/731-2626
http://www.grandopening.com

Toys in Babeland, store and catalog
707 East Pike Street
Seattle, WA 98122
206/328-2914
800/658-9119
http://www.babeland.com

Xandria Collection, catalog
Lawrence Research Group
165 Valley Drive
Brisbane, CA 94005
415/468-3812
800/242-2823
http://www.xandria.com

Informational web sites:
Good Vibrations
http://www.goodvibes.com
Offers information, trivia, shopping and
an online antique vibrator museum.

SIECUS
http://www.siecus.org
The Sex Information and Education
Council of the U.S. offers extensive
information and bibliographies on a
wide variety of sexually-related topics.

Society for Human Sexuality
http://www.sexuality.org
An extensive online library of sexual
materials and information, maintained
by students at Seattle's University of
Washington.

About the Author

Cathy Winks worked for ten stimulating years at Good Vibrations. In the store, she sold vibrators, books and videos, while behind the scenes she reviewed and selected sex toys and videos. She also played a pivotal role in the remarkable growth of the business, a worker-owned cooperative since 1992. She is the author of *The Good Vibrations Guide: Adult Videos*, and co-author of *The New Good Vibrations Guide to Sex* and *The Woman's Guide to Sex on the Web*.

Selected Titles from DOWN THERE PRESS

_____ **The Good Vibrations Guide: The G-Spot,** Cathy Winks. How to find and enjoy the elusive pleasure spot and understand female ejaculation. $7.00

_____ **The Big Book of Masturbation: From Angst to Zeal**, Martha Cornog. "...amazing...made my jaw drop open...best reference..." Susie Bright. $22.00

_____ **Anal Pleasure & Health, rev. 3rd ed.,** Jack Morin, Ph.D. The definitive guide discusses techniques, power dynamics and identifying sex-positive health practitioners for women and men. $18.00

_____ **Good Vibrations: The New Complete Guide to Vibrators, rev. 4th ed.,** Joani Blank with Ann Whidden. Everything you want to know about vibrators. $8.50

_____ **Exhibitionism for the Shy: Show Off, Dress Up and Talk Hot**, Carol Queen. Discover your erotic inner persona with this Firecracker Award Finalist. $12.50

_____ **The Leather Daddy and The Femme,** Carol Queen. No-holds-barred, over-the-top liaisons, from the mistress of sexual storytelling, with three new chapters. $13.50

_____ **Any 2 People, Kissing**, Kate Dominic. A tantalizing exploration of power exchange and sex play in tales that tickle and entice libidos from queer to straight. $12.50

_____ **Herotica® 6,** Marcy Sheiner, editor. Hot sex in committed relationships. *Foreword Magazine* Erotic Book of the Year. $12.50

_____ **Herotica®: A Collection of Women's Erotic Fiction, 10th Anniversary Edition,** Susie Bright, editor. The underground classic that launched a genre! $11.00

_____ **Sex Toy Tales,** Anne Semans and Cathy Winks, editors. Tasty tales incorporating a variety of imaginative sexual accessories. $12.50

_____ **Photo Sex**, David Steinberg, editor. Fine art sexual photography brings a new dimension to sexual pleasure, with 115 carefully selected duotones. $35.00

_____ **Erotic by Nature**, David Steinberg, editor. A luscious volume of photos, line drawings, prose and poetry for, by and of women and men. Clothbound. $45.00

_____ **I Am My Lover**, Joani Blank, editor. Artful duotone and B&W photos of twelve women pleasuring themselves. Lambda Literary Award nominee. $25.00

_____ **Femalia**, Joani Blank, editor. Thirty-two stunning color photographs of vulvas by four photographers, for aesthetic enjoyment and edification. $14.50

_____ **Still Doing It: Women & Men Over 60 Write About Their Sexuality**, Joani Blank, editor. Proof-positive that sex never has to end. *Independent Publisher* Award. $12.50

_____ **First Person Sexual,** Joani Blank, editor. Women and men share the myriad ways they experience solo sex. *Small Press* Book Award Winner. $14.50

_____ Good Vibrations Catalog. Sex toys, books, videos, massage oils, safer sex supplies.

Buy these books from your local bookstore, call toll-free at **1-800-289-8423,** log on to **www.goodvibes.com,** or mail a copy of this page with your name and street address to:

Down There Press, 938 Howard St., #101, San Francisco CA 94103

Please include $6.95 shipping costs for the first book ordered and $2.00 for each additional book. California residents please add sales tax.

Name_____

UPS Street Address_____

_____ZIP_____

_____

MasterCard/Visa/Amex/Discover   Exp. Date